THE DOG WHO SMELLED DANGER

As they entered the clearing, Smoky growled softly and looked toward the cabin. Paying no attention, Tom walked up on the porch. He stopped in his tracks.

Somebody had been here since he left. Smoky's growl should have given him warning of that. Tom stared at the paper that was stuck in the door, pulled it out, and read it twice.

> There's enough people around here now. Get out within forty-eight hours or take what's coming to you.

The signature was a drawing of a black elk!

Bantam Skylark Books by Jim Kjelgaard
Ask your bookseller for the books you have missed

A Nose for
Trouble

Jim Kjelgaard

A BANTAM SKYLARK BOOK®
TORONTO · NEW YORK · LONDON · SYDNEY · AUCKLAND

*This low-priced Bantam Book
has been completely reset in a type face
designed for easy reading, and was printed
from new plates. It contains the complete
text of the original hard-cover edition.*
NOT ONE WORD HAS BEEN OMITTED.

RL 6, 012-014

A NOSE FOR TROUBLE

*A Bantam Book / published by arrangement with
Holiday House Inc.*

PRINTING HISTORY
Holiday House edition published September 1949
13 printings through February 1971
Bantam Skylark edition / September 1982
2nd printing . . . October 1984
3rd printing . . . April 1986

ISBN 0-553-15456-7

Published simultaneously in the United States and Canada

*Bantam Books are published by Bantam Books, Inc. Its trade-
mark, consisting of the words "Bantam Books" and the por-
trayal of a rooster, is Registered in U.S. Patent and Trademark
Office and in other countries. Marca Registrada. Bantam
Books, Inc., 666 Fifth Avenue, New York, New York 10103.*

PRINTED IN THE UNITED STATES OF AMERICA

O   12 11 10 9 8 7 6 5 4 3

For Eddy and Karen

Contents

1
Homecoming

Tom Rainse sat up in his day-coach seat as the train began the long, switchback climb over Tanner's Mountain. He peered eagerly through the smudged window. It seemed to him that he had left here only yesterday, instead of five years ago.

When the train reached the mountain's top, he gazed down a long slope toward a clearing and a town in the bottom of a valley. The town was Hilldale. Five years ago, just after his father died, he had boarded the train there to join a wild stampede to western gold fields.

Tom leaned forward, narrowing his eyes and focusing them on the hillside pasture at the upper end of the town. Enclosed by barbed wire, half a hundred horses grazed in the sloping pasture. They were of all colors and weights, from heavy work beasts to lithe saddle stock.

1

They seemed like a lot of horses, for Hilldale. Tom kept his eyes on them as the train sped down the mountain toward the town. Suddenly his glance was arrested by one horse standing alone.

A black and white pinto, it stood on the very top of the pasture hill. Trim and graceful, it held its head high against the wind that ruffled its silvery mane. Tom's eyes remained on it until the descending train had passed, then he twisted in his seat so he could continue to watch. The pinto did not move.

There were all kinds of horses in the mountains, Tom reflected, but not too many good ones ever found their way to Hilldale. The pinto looked good to Tom: fast, tough, and agile. Still, he had no reason to think of horses now. He would be back in Hilldale for a short time only.

The train puffed to a sliding halt in front of the town's small station. Tom pulled his canvas pack from the rack above his seat and made his way to the door. He stepped down on the station platform, and sniffed the clean air hungrily.

He had seen a lot of country since he had left his native hills. He had been through burning deserts and up snow-capped peaks. But this region was his home; he had been born back in the mountains that surrounded the little town. Now he had returned, five years older and the possessor of a few hundred dollars he had grubbed out of hard-to-find gold pockets.

The only person in sight was a buck-toothed attendant pushing a baggage cart.

2

"Say," Tom asked him, "who owns that herd of horses I saw from the train?"

"What'd you want to know for?" the attendant demanded suspiciously.

"I might want to rent a horse."

"Don't rent one off'n Fred Larsen," the attendant replied gloomily. "Such of his hosses as ain't got the heaves are wind-broke, or spavined, or somethin' else. Besides, he won't rent you none."

"Thanks."

Tom shouldered his pack and strode up the dusty street, toward the corrals he had seen from the train. Hilldale had changed considerably. New buildings had been erected and some of the old ones had even been painted. Still a sleepy mountain town, it had begun to show at least a few signs of activity. Most of the people were strangers, and Tom made no effort to find anyone he knew. The mountains, not the town, were his home, and the mountain folk his only close friends. If he could get even a reasonably decent horse under him, he could reach his father's old cabin by nightfall. Tomorrow he'd ride over to see the Tollivers and get whatever news there might be.

He came to the pasture, and carefully looked over the grazing horses. The baggage attendant had been right. There was nothing to recommend any of them, that he could see. They were mostly pack horses, and some of them looked as though they might collapse of their own weight any second.

He looked at the top of the hill, and saw the black and

3

white pinto still standing there. It was no thoroughbred, but its trim lines suggested a strong dash of Arab in its mingled ancestry. Tom twitched his nose, and fell to a disinterested study of a lanky bay mare that stood near the fence. He stole another glance at the pinto. The black and white horse was alert, watching him, following his every move. Tom dropped his pack and leaned over the fence.

From the corner of his eye he saw a big, dishevelled man emerge from the small barn at the foot of the hill and come toward him, scowling. Tom decided that the scowl was probably permanent. His face was heavily lined, marked with a strong crosshatch of red veins. Even his eyes were red. The approaching stranger looked anything but friendly.

"Who are you and what do you want?" he growled when he came near.

Tom swung to face him. "Are these your horses?"

"Yeah. What about it?"

"I'd like to rent one."

"Ain't got none for rent."

"No?" Tom pointed to a group of horses that were milling near the fence. "You don't use all of them for your own packing, do you, Larsen?"

Fred Larsen glanced at the horses that bore marks chafed by pack saddles, then looked keenly at Tim.

"I do some packin'," he admitted, "but I still ain't got no horses for rent. I'll sell you one."

"Wasn't figuring to buy. I'll be in only a few days."

"Where you goin'?"

"Back in the mountains."

4

"Pretty wild country, mister. Know folks there?"

"Could be."

Tom stifled a growing annoyance. Five years ago any stranger could have come into Hilldale, rented a horse, and gone where he willed without question. Now, for some reason, this horse dealer was getting almighty curious.

"Do you want to sell that pinto?" he asked shortly.

"Dunno about that one. It's a mighty good horse," Larsen evaded.

Tom grinned. The pinto was for sale, but at the highest possible price. That was the kind of horse trading Tom understood. He stooped down for his pack, and shouldered it again.

"Well, keep it then. I'm used to walking."

The big man blinked his bloodshot eyes. "I'd sell him, but I'd have to get my price."

"What's your price?"

"A hundred and fifty dollars."

"I'll give you fifty."

"That ain't no pack horse, mister! Look at him."

"I can get a lot of horse for a hundred and fifty dollars."

Fred Larsen showed his teeth in a yellow grin. "That pinto *is* a lot of horse, stranger."

"I'll give you seventy-five."

"Hundred and twenty-five, cash."

Tom took out his poke, and shook a twenty-dollar gold piece into the palm of his hand.

"I'll toss you for it. Heads, I get him for seventy-five. Tails, I give you a hundred and twenty-five."

The other considered for a moment. "All right, on one condition. You pay me cash right now, and no goin' back on the deal."

"I might not like it," Tom said mildly, "if a wind-broken horse was unloaded on me."

"I'll guarantee that pinto is sound as your double eagle, and stand behind that."

"Good enough."

Tom flipped the gold piece. It glittered brightly in the sun, and fell on the scuffed earth beside the pasture fence. Fred Larsen bent over to look.

"Heads," he conceded sourly. He picked up the coin, and suspiciously turned it over.

Tom laughed as he counted out two more twenty dollar gold pieces, a ten, and a five-dollar bill. Then he balanced his poke in his hand.

"How about a saddle and bridle?"

Fred Larsen jerked a stubby thumb toward the barn. "I got three stock saddles and half a dozen bridles in there. Take your pick, along with a blanket, for fifty dollars."

"Let's see 'em."

Larsen led him back into the barn, and Tom looked at the three saddles on a rack. They were good enough, as were the leather bridles and blankets, and Tom counted out fifty dollars more. He shouldered the saddle, hung the bridle on it, and with the blanket in his other hand climbed the hill to the black and white pinto. Larsen leaned on the fence and watched.

He approached slowly but confidently, making no swift moves that would alarm the horse. His eyes roved over its trim, clean lines, and his heart warmed. The pinto would be fast and quick on its feet, and its well-developed chest bespoke endurance.

As Tom came near, the horse extended a soft muzzle to snuffle him over. Tom scratched its ears.

"Pete," he said softly. "From now on your name is Pete. If you're as good as you look, I've really got me a horse!"

He slipped the bit into the pinto's mouth and strapped the bridle on. Holding the reins in his left hand, he laid the blanket on the horse's back, threw the saddle over it, and tightened the cinch. Pete made no objection, and followed Tom willingly when he led him down the hill and through the gate that Fred Larsen had opened.

"Well, mister, he's your horse now," said the dealer, closing the gate. "Let's see you ride him."

Tom put his left foot into the stirrup, and threw his right leg over the saddle. The world seemed to explode. The pinto reared, then came stiffly down on his front legs, only to throw his hindquarters into the air. Almost unseated, Tom tightened his knees and hung on.

He knew now why Fred Larsen had insisted that there should be no return after the deal was closed. The pinto was gentle enough—until someone tried to ride him.

He was bucking now, thudding about with racking jars that cracked through Tom's spine and up into his skull. Tom held a light rein, letting Pete have his head and do his worst. If he was ever going to ride the horse, it had to be now.

The pinto gave a wild sidewise lunge, twisting his back as he did so. Tom grimly held his seat. He had ridden pitching horses before, but never one like this. No horse he had ever ridden had such agility.

Three minutes later it was all over. The pinto suddenly stopped bucking and stood still, his sides heaving. Pete had met his master, and acknowledged it. Tom reined him lightly to the left, then to the right, and turned him back to where the dealer stood with mouth agape.

"Gosh!" he gasped. "Goshamighty!"

"Good horse," Tom said calmly. "Little frisky, though."

"Frisky! Mister, every man in the mountains has had a crack at that hoss, but you're the first as ever rode him to a standstill!"

Tom laughed, swung from the saddle, and picked up his pack. The pinto stood quietly as Tom lifted the pack to his back, tied it behind the saddle, and again mounted. Pete quivered, then relaxed and stood contentedly stamping his feet while Tom turned in the saddle to wave at the astonished dealer.

"So long. And thanks for the bargain."

Tom trotted his new horse back into Hilldale, hiding his amusement at the men who turned to stare; evidently the pinto had a reputation as an outlaw. Tom stopped only long enough to buy a few supplies, then headed out of town again.

They were soon out of the clearings and into deep forest, the trim little horse walking effortlessly up the mountain road. As Tom leaned forward to pat the pinto's neck, he grinned at his own impetuosity. He had returned to his home country intending to stay just long enough to renew old acquaintances and pick up his belongings. Now, before he had been back an hour, he found himself the owner of a horse he didn't need. Maybe he'd sell him to Bill Tolliver when he left. Bill liked fast horses.

He turned from the road down a shaded woods trail, and reined up to look curiously at the many hoof marks in the soft dirt. Some were old and some fresh; horses apparently traveled this way regularly. That was unusual. Times must have changed; in the old days this trail was seldom used.

Far off, muted by distance and the intervening forest, a rifle shot rang out. Tom sat still. There was no second shot and no other sound save those common to the wilderness. He frowned, puzzled. Who would be shooting up here in this late summer season? Nobody used to live in this section. Tom urged the pinto into a trot.

A half mile farther on, by a branch trail, he saw the fresh tracks of a shod horse. Again Tom reined Pete to a halt, bending over his neck and looking down at the trail. The tracks were far apart; the horse had been galloping. And they were very recent. Tom glanced down the branch trail from which the galloping horse had come, then went on.

Letting Pete walk slowly, he continued to study the tracks. Presently Pete bent his ears forward and nickered softly.

Tom raised his head to see a man with a revolver in his hand step from behind a tree. He was a tall man, broadshouldered, and with a shock of unruly red hair. His denim shirt was soaked with sweat, and there was a

9

bloody furrow across the right cheek. It might, Tom decided, have been slashed by a sharp branch—or nicked by a bullet. He couldn't tell.

"What do you want here?" the stranger demanded brusquely.

Tom sat silently, resentful of both tone and manner. He used to travel these mountains with nobody inquiring as to where or why. Now it seemed to be everyone's business.

"I'm trying to mind my own affairs," he answered.

"I asked what you're doing here," the stranger repeated.

"Look, my name is Tom Rainse. I've been away for five years. I just got back to Hilldale this morning. All I aim to do is head for my cabin down on Rainse's Creek. I don't know what anybody else is doing and I don't care. Now stand aside."

"Where'd you get the horse?"

"Bought it. Now look here—"

"All right, Rainse. Go on."

The man holstered his revolver and stood silently aside. Tom clucked to Pete, and without looking back rode on down the trail.

He had a lot to think about. The shot he had heard had been from a rifle, and this man was carrying only a revolver, which was odd enough in itself. If the shot he had heard had been intended for the redheaded man in the trail, then it had nearly killed him. Who would shoot at him? Why had the man shown himself at all? Where did all the hoof marks come from? Something about which he knew nothing was certainly going on in his once-peaceful mountains. He'd better see Bill Tolliver tomorrow and find out.

Nine miles from Hilldale they came to another branch trail, and Tom swung his mount up it into a forested valley. As they came to a spring-fed trout stream across the trail, a splash of sunlight revealed a clearing ahead. They broke into the clearing and Tom pulled up the pinto.

"We're home, Pete," Tom said happily. "How do you like it?"

A sturdy log cabin occupied the center of the clearing. Beyond it was a small barn with a little corral attached. At the end of the clearing, where it pitched four feet over a shelf of rock, Rainse's Creek was white spray. A couple of deer that had been feeding fled silently back into the forest. But Tom scarcely glanced at them. He was staring at the cabin.

He had left it five years ago. It should have been tumbledown and porcupine chewed. But it was in good repair. Somebody had certainly been living in it, and recently. Well, there was nothing wrong with that, Tom reflected as he dismounted. The cabin had been empty, and it would do no harm to have it occupied, as long as the occupants had not abused their privilege.

"Besides, they should have left wood behind," Tom murmured to Pete. "Then I won't have to cut any."

Tom unlashed the pack, swung it down, and left it in front of the cabin while he led Pete to the corral. The barn door sagged on rusting hinges. Whoever had lived in the cabin had evidently not used the barn. Tom opened the corral gate, led Pete inside, unsaddled and unbridled him, and rubbed him down. Then he left the black and white horse contentedly cropping grass while he returned to the cabin.

Picking up his pack, he stepped inside and looked around. He had been wrong. It was not a matter of who *had* been living in his cabin, but who *was* living in it!

Well, whoever it was, he was a fairly neat housekeeper, Tom admitted. The place was reasonably clean and quite livable. There was wood in the wood box, and kindling on top of the wood. The kerosene lamps were half filled. There was flour, salt, sugar, half a can of lard, and dried apples in the pantry. His blankets, which he had left tied in a pack suspended from the rafters, were neatly made up on the bed. Tom had left his guns, fishing tackle, and all valuable articles with old Bill Tolliver, so he did not have to wonder about them.

Tom stood in the middle of the floor, staring about him in bewilderment. Who could have moved in so calmly and made himself free with Tom's possessions? True, he had been away a long time, and no one knew when he was coming back. It was probably one of his friends—maybe somebody whose cabin had burned. Tom shrugged. This was just another homecoming mystery to ask Bill Tolliver about. Meantime, he was hungry.

He unlaced his pack, stowing his personal articles in the closet but keeping out a length of fishing line and his box of tackle. That tackle had been a godsend more than once when he had ventured into lonely places without adequate supplies, and now it would serve again. Twilight shadows were gathering over the clearing when he stepped outside with the line and tackle box in his hand.

Pete, who had eaten as much as he could hold, nickered from the corral. Tom talked softly to the black and white horse as he walked toward a stand of willows near the creek. With his clasp knife he cut a lithe wand, attached the line to it, and tied a hook on the line. He kicked a rotten stump apart, found a handful of white grubs, baited his hook, and cast. Within ten minutes he had four trout, all he could eat for supper and breakfast.

After supper, Tom sat on the porch while darkness closed over the mountains. No one came, and he heard nothing but the familiar sounds of the forest and the brook. In spite of all his unanswered questions, he was supremely happy just to be back. The whippoorwills were singing their night songs, and Pete was a shapeless mass in the corral, when he finally went to bed.

2

Smoky

Tom was up with the dawn, and breakfasted on the remaining trout and some soda biscuits. Then he saddled Pete and started up the trail that led away from the far end of the clearing. He wanted to waste no time in seeing Bill Tolliver.

After a stiff hour's climb they came out on top of the mountain, and Tom stopped to let the pinto breathe.

The year before he had left the mountains, a forest fire which he had helped to fight had roared through here. It had destroyed everything in its path, even swallowing seventy-foot pines at one gulp. Now the burn was growing back up. Huckleberry brush grew profusely, with here and there a patch of fast-growing aspens scattered among it. Pete flicked his ears forward and looked in-

14

tently toward a patch of aspens. Tom followed the horse's gaze.

He thought at first that he was looking at a stump, one of many charred souvenirs left by the fire. But it was an odd-looking stump. Tom rode a bit nearer, although the pinto seemed reluctant, and was blowing nervously through his nostrils.

It was not a stump, but a great black boar with a massive chest, lean paunch, and legs built for speed. Long tushes protruded from its mouth, and its little pig eyes stared steadily at the man on the horse. Then, so suddenly that Tom could not be sure his eyes followed it at all, the monster faded into the underbrush.

Tom walked Pete slowly forward. He had been born in the mountains, and in earliest boyhood had learned that most wild animals would flee at the sight of a man. But this thing, instead of running, had faced him. In fact, it had seemed almost on the verge of charging him. Tom tried to fight back the cold chill that traveled up his spine. The boar was a tremendous creature, as big as the black bears that roamed the mountains, and much more deadly.

Still shaken, Tom dismounted where the creature had stood. He found wide, cloven hoof marks in the soft earth, the biggest he had ever seen. When he rose, he looked nervously about in spite of himself. An unarmed man on foot wouldn't stand a chance should such a thing attack him. Fighting back the coldness in the pit of his stomach, Tom remounted and put Pete to a swift trot that carried them across the burn and among the trees at the other side.

As soon as he was again among trees he felt more at ease, and slowed the pinto to a walk. Probably the boar wouldn't have charged him at all; few wild beasts deliberately attacked men. Maybe he had surprised it, and the creature was waiting to see what he would do before making its own escape. That must have been the answer.

The trail angled among big pines, down the sloping face of the mountain. Far below, Tom saw another clearing and heard hounds that had already scented them begin to bay. He let Pete trot toward the Tolliver clearing, his mind at rest.

He had always liked old Bill Tolliver. A typical mountain man, wise in the ways of the woods, Bill had taught Tom much of what he knew, including marksmanship. Bill was a dead shot. It was he who had bought a single box of twenty cartridges for his big rifle, and killed eighteen deer and two bears with them. Store-bought ammunition cost too much to waste, he had explained modestly. Tom smiled at the recollection.

As they reached the clearing at the bottom of the mountain, Bill's hound pack surged about them. Tom saw Twig, the aging leader of Bill's pack, and Jerry. The rest were dogs Tom had never seen before. That was not surprising. The bears and cats that old Bill liked to hunt were fierce fighters that could work damage to any pack of hounds. In five years most hunters of such game had an entirely new pack.

Then Tom saw another dog that had leisurely followed the rest.

It was a large, tawny hound, smoke-gray in color. One of its dangling ears had been ripped and was almost healed. Tom looked wonderingly at it. Its outward conformation was similar to the Plott hounds that made up old Bill's pack, but it was not a Plott hound. Its jowls were very heavy, and overhung the lower jaw in leathery folds. On the sad-looking face, tan relieved the hound's smoky-gray color.

The hounds that had already snuffled around the pinto's feet drifted slowly back toward the Tolliver cabin. Only the sad-looking dog remained. Tom dismounted.

"Hi, Smoky," he said gravely, snapping his fingers.

The smoke-colored hound trotted up and snuffled him over. He raised his head, and to Tom's surprise, reared to be petted. Wagging his tail, he pushed his nose toward Tom's face. Grasping him by the front legs, Tom set the big dog gently down on the grass.

"You like me, eh?" he laughed.

As he led the pinto toward the cabin, the rest of the hounds rose to bay at them, and two growled forward. The smoke-colored dog padded contentedly by Tom's side. When he came near, the two belligerent hounds drew back. Tom grinned. Obviously the big hound was not one to pick fights, but just as plainly he was able to hold his own. Then Tom looked up at the man who stood in the doorway.

Bill Tolliver was short and broad, stocky without being fat. A mane of pure white hair crowned his head and a flowing white beard fell over his barrel chest. But when he came forward his walk was the easy, light stride of a boy. He extended an immense hand.

"Tawm Rainse!"

"Hello, Bill."

17

"It's good to see you, boy! It's been a long time. Say! Ain't that Fred Larsen's outlaw you're ridin'?"

"Pete's no outlaw," Tom grinned. "He just had to find the right owner."

"Is that so?" Bill Tolliver rumbled enviously. "I'd have bought the critter myself, but I couldn't stay on him. Come along, boy. Mother Tolliver and Elaine will be right glad to see you."

"Elaine?"

"Yancey's woman," Tolliver explained. "Yancey was killed by a fallin' tree, two years back. Elaine and baby Sue are bidin' here with us."

Tom nodded silently, knowing that words were futile. Yancey had been Bill's only son.

They turned the black and white pinto into the corral with Bill Tolliver's horses. The smoke-colored hound followed. As they walked back toward the house, the dog wagged his tail at a golden-haired little girl who was playing in the yard. The toddler reached out, took both the dog's ears in her fists, and yanked. The dog wagged his tail harder, and made no effort to pull away from the youngster.

"Where'd you get the good-natured hound, Bill?" Tom asked. "And what is he?"

"Ain't he the dog?" Bill Tolliver said. "They had a bloodhound in here 'bout a year or so past. Tryin' to track down a man, they was. They never caught him, but that bloodhound sure left his own tracks behind. Out of old Twig, that Smoky dog is."

"Then his name *is* Smoky?"

"Sure. What else could you call him with a color like that?"

"He any good?"

"He's smart, and he's got a nose second to none, but he ain't no pack dog. Got his own ideas about what he'll do and won't do. Friendly cuss with humans, but he can lick any two dogs in the pack. Reckon I'll have to get rid of him."

"Sell him to me."

"I'll give him to you, Tawn, if you don't aim to keep but one dog. Smoky won't run with any others. And dogged if I know whether he's a game hound or a man-hunter. He can't seem to make up his mind."

"I'll find out," Tom told him. "It's a deal."

Bill Tolliver pushed the door open and Tom followed him into the neat cabin. Yancey Tolliver's pretty widow, Elaine, turned around and smiled shyly. Bill's booming voice filled the cabin.

"Here's Tawm Rainse, Mother! Got in last night."

Mrs. Tolliver, a pleasant, graying woman, looked up from the stove.

"Land sakes, young'un, let me look at you! I swear to goodness, the mountains have been plumb lonesome 'thout a Rainse around! Dinner will be on in a few minutes."

"But I had a big breakfast," Tom protested.

"I bet 'twas a man's breakfast," Mrs. Tolliver sniffed. "Trout and biscuits, or I miss my guess. Anyhow, I've yet to see the man who can't eat two meals runnin'. Sit tight."

The smoke-colored dog appeared in the doorway, and turned his head expectantly. Sue Tolliver toddled across the porch, fastened both hands in the skin of the big hound's neck, and held tightly. Slowly, careful not to upset the little girl, Smoky walked into the cabin. Sue hung on until she was well inside, then released the dog and climbed up on a low bench.

His duty done, Smoky padded across the floor to throw himself at Tom's feet. He wagged his tail a couple of times, gave a great sigh, and went to sleep.

Mrs. Tolliver laughed. "He likes you, Tom."

"Good thing," her husband observed. "He's Tawm's dog now. I gave Smoky to him."

"Well, I'm glad he's going to somebody who knows a good hound from a broody hen. Smoky's my favorite among all the dogs, Tom, even if he doesn't run with the pack. Now stand aside, you men, and let us get some food on. Everything is just about ready."

She and Elaine loaded the table with a venison roast, fluffy mashed potatoes, green peas from the Tolliver's garden, feather-light biscuits with golden butter and wild honey. On top of the oven a big, steamy-crusted strawberry pie was waiting. Mrs. Tolliver filled the cups with smoking hot coffee, and put the pot back on the stove.

"All right, young'un, sit and eat," she told Tom. "And let me see you eat like you should."

As they sat down, little Sue left her bench, walked over to her grandfather, and climbed into his lap. Tom watched them. Like most mountaineers, Bill Tolliver was quiet and closemouthed, not given to showing his emotions. But now there seemed to be something especially tender about him, as he curled his great arm about his tiny granddaughter, something that went very deep. Sue, Tom decided, had taken Yancey's place. She had filled the aching void which the death of his son had left in the old man.

Tolliver felt Tom's eyes on him, glanced up, then looked down at his granddaughter's silky head.

"Cute little tyke, ain't she?" he mumbled in embarrassment. "Well, Tawm, how'd you find everythin' at Rainse's Creek? Old place look familiar?"

"Not exactly," Tom replied. "Somebody's been using the cabin—still is, by the looks of things."

The news was obviously a surprise to all of them.

"Wonder who it is?" asked Mrs. Tolliver. "If 'twas any of the mountain folks, we'd a-known it. Who could it be, Bill?"

The old man shook his head. "I dunno, Mother. I ain't been over thataway in some time."

He did not look at Tom as he spoke. Maybe he knew more than he admitted, but didn't want to talk in front of the women, Tom reflected. He'd wait until they were alone.

He gave himself over to the venison roast, filled his plate again, and ate a second helping. When Mrs. Tolliver placed a huge wedge of pie beside him, he ate that too. Then he pushed himself back with a contented sigh.

"Gosh! That was good. Didn't know I was so hungry."

"You had enough?" Mrs. Tolliver inquired solicitously.

"All I can eat, and then some! But I will take another cup of coffee."

"Say, Bill," he went on, passing his cup, "when I crossed the burn above our cabin this morning, I ran across a wild boar as big as sin and twice as ugly."

"Did he tackle you?"

"No, but for a minute I thought he was going to."

"We call him the Black Devil," Bill Tolliver said, "and there's no tellin' where he come from. Genuine Rooshian wild boar he is, and smarter'n any six foxes in the mountains. I'm just waitin' for a shot at him."

"If he's bad, why don't you get him?"

"I tried, and it cost me three good hounds. Some of the others have tried, too. We don't get him 'cause we can't. He's too smart for us. Only reason you got a sight of him today, I swear, was on account he knew you didn't have a rifle."

"Suppose you two go outside and hunt your boars on the porch," Mrs. Tolliver interrupted good-naturedly. "We've got work to do."

"I'm pretty good with dishes—" Tom offered.

Mrs. Tolliver sniffed. "As if I'd let a man mess around my kitchen! Go along now, and talk your hearts out."

Bill Tolliver pushed back his chair. "When Mother speaks, it's best to pay heed. Come on, Tawm."

As they went out on the porch, Smoky got up and padded behind them. When they sat on the step, the dog flopped down beside Tom, his nose hanging over the edge so that his dangling ears nearly reached the ground.

"Looks like you got yourself a dog, Tawm, and the dog sure figures he's got him a man."

22

"Yeah," Tom replied absently, scratching Smoky's ears. "Bill, what's going on around here?"

"I knew you'd smelled somethin'," Bill replied, his face darkening, "and you've got a right to know." He was silent a moment, gazing off across the clearing.

"The law's part of it. They've upped and made a lot of foolish rules 'bout what a man can and can't shoot, and when he can do it. Then they sent their fool game warden in here to make the rules stick. Me, I been shootin' what I pleased for the past fifty years, and I aim to keep right on. I like to eat regular. Always did."

"What else?" Tom asked quietly.

Bill was silent again, groping for words. Smoky wrinkled his nose and interestedly followed the progress of a black beetle along the ground.

"Well, besides that piddlin' little game warden, we got more things the mountains can do without. You know I ain't never wasted game. But there are some as do."

"Who are they?"

"I don't know right off," the old man admitted. "Whoever heads the thing calls himself the Black Elk. Seems like a bunch of 'em are either shootin' or buyin' game, or both, and packin' it out to sell to hotels and such-like. And it ain't healthy to be too nosy about what's goin' on."

"What are you going to do about it?"

"Nothin'," Bill Tolliver grunted. "I ain't scared of this Black Elk, like some folks. But I still figure a body's business is his own. even if I don't like the way this bunch is doin' things. Tawm, I found where they kil't five deer at one salt lick, and three of 'em was does."

23

"Why don't you tell this game warden about it?"

"Help a game warden? I druther cut off my right arm. Nope! I'll just mind my own business, same as I always have."

"How are the rest of the mountain folks taking it?"

"Some are scared, like I said, but most are sittin' tight. They dunno what to make of anythin', what with these new rules, and this here Black Elk bustin' 'em by the hayrick load."

Tom was silent, knowing the uselessness of trying to pump more information out of a mountain man than he was willing to give. And Bill had talked a lot, for him. The whole atmosphere in the mountains seemed one of fear and worry. So game law had come among the mountaineers. They had been told that their hunting grounds, used by themselves and their fathers and grandfathers before them, were no longer free. However, few of the mountain people had ever taken more game than they could use, and there had always been plenty. Now some unknown man or men, who were killing for markets, had moved in. Knowing that the mountaineers would resent indiscriminate slaughter, this Black Elk, as he called himself, had apparently resorted to threats.

"There's got to be a showdown, Bill," Tom said at last. "This can't keep up."

"I'll be here when it comes," the old man answered calmly. "You stayin' in the mountains for long?"

"I wasn't going to, but it looks as though things might get right exciting. I'll stick around for a while."

"Glad to hear it, boy. I'll get your rifle and a fishin' rod

24

for you. Rest of your stuff I'll tote in on a pack horse next time I happen by. Got enough grub?"

"Enough for now, Bill. And thanks for everything. Guess I'll head back for home."

While Bill was getting his rifle and rod, Tom sat where he was, thinking hard. He was disturbed by what the old man had told him, and confused by what more he could guess. Although Bill hadn't said so, he suspected that some of the mountaineers must be working with this mysterious Black Elk. Outsiders would need men who knew where game was most plentiful. Who could they be? Did Bill know?

When the old man reappeared, Mrs. Tolliver followed him out of the door.

"Land sakes, young'un, you haven't even told us what you've been doing all these years," she protested. "You can't go now."

"I'll be back, Mother," Tom promised. "It'll be a good excuse for a free meal."

Bill handed him his rifle, a handful of cartridges, and his fishing rod, and walked out to the corral with him. Smoky followed them.

"I dunno who's been usin' your cabin, Tawm," he warned, "but you'd best find out. That Smoky dog will smell anybody comin', but watch out that he don't wag his fool tail off welcomin' strangers!"

Smoky raised his head at the sound of his name. His drooping jowls made his face look so sad that Tom burst out laughing.

"You've hurt his feelings, Bill. Now he'll be glad to leave you."

"Mebbe so," Bill grinned, "but I doubt he'll follow you without you got him on a lead. I'll fetch one."

Bill disappeared into the barn, and Tom walked along the corral to the gate. On his side of the fence the black and white pinto detached himself from the herd and followed eagerly. When Tom entered the pasture the trim little horse came up to him at once, and stood quietly while he was being saddled. Tom led him out, and was loading the rifle when Bill Tolliver brought Smoky up on a fifteen-foot hank of rope. He handed the end of the leash to Tom.

"There you are, boy. Come again when you take a notion. We're glad to see you any time."

"Thanks, Bill. I'll ease by now and again."

Tom slung the rifle and rod across the saddle, mounted, and swung Pete toward the trail, letting the reins hang slack. Pete trotted willingly along, and Tom nodded in satisfaction. The black and white pinto was an intelligent horse. He had been over the trail from the Rainse clearing to the Tollivers' only once, but he seemed to sense that they were returning the same way, and asked no guidance.

For a moment Smoky hung back against the leash, looking questioningly over his shoulder. Tom reined Pete to a halt and spoke to the big dog.

"Come on, boy. Don't be worried. You're going with me."

The tawny hound looked at him, wagged his tail, and then trotted contentedly beside Pete.

Tom looked appraisingly at him. Dogs were as different as humans in their reactions, and Smoky was def-

26

initely a rugged individualist. He wouldn't run with the pack, and he insisted on having his rights respected. But such dogs often turned out to be the finest possible companions to those who wanted only one dog. Smoky had already demonstrated his willingness to meet any advance more than halfway, and he seemed to have taken more than a casual liking to Tom.

When they entered the forest, Pete began to climb without hesitation. He picked a sure way among the boulders, easing his pace where the going was steepest, so he would not wind himself. Smoky ranged ahead at the end of the leash, snuffling here and there, but always maintaining his distance so that he did not interfere with the horse. Obviously the tawny hound was used to running with horses. Satisfied, Tom gave himself up to his thoughts.

He remembered these mountains as a friendly place where no one ever had to carry a gun unless he was hunting. Of course there had always been the usual quota of wild and unruly natives, but they were seldom vicious. Now, apparently, all that was changed. The mountains were in the grip of some gang or other, and even old Bill Tolliver trod mighty warily. Who was the Black Elk? Who was helping him? What were they doing with the wild life they slaughtered? Did the occupant of his cabin figure in it?

Tom came to the burn at the top of the mountain, and let Pete's reins hang slack while he braced the fishing rod against the pommel. Rifle in hand, he raised himself in the stirrups and looked about for signs of the boar. Seeing nothing, he pulled Smoky over to the tracks he had seen that morning. The big hound snuffled about obediently, then looked up. He seemed to be asking what he was supposed to do about it. Tom laughed at his sad, reproachful face, then clucked to Pete and started down the slope toward his cabin. He didn't know just what he had expected the hound to do himself, he admitted.

They were still a quarter of a mile from the cabin when Smoky stopped. He stood with one front paw curled back, as though he were pointing birds. A soft growl rumbled in his throat. Tom bent forward, trying in vain to see through the trees that overhung the trail. He whistled softly to himself. It was almost incredible to think that the hound could smell the cabin from this distance. Could it be something else?

Tom rode slowly forward, rifle raised and his eyes on Smoky. The tawny hound strained forward, pulling on the leash and testing the wind currents as he advanced. Whoever or whatever he smelled *must* be at the cabin. Then Tom rode into the clearing.

The first thing he saw was a black and white pinto that might have been Pete's twin, tied to the porch railing. A man sat beside the horse, swinging his feet. Pete nickered a greeting to the other horse and was answered. The man looked toward them, and stood up.

It was the same stocky, red-haired man who had stopped Tom in the trail yesterday!

3

Challenge

As Tom rode up, he noticed that the man had changed his denim shirt for a clean wool one, and had treated the cut on his face with iodine. He was still packing his revolver, though, and a rifle leaned against the railing of the porch.

"Hello, Rainse," the stranger greeted him. "I thought I'd better wait for you and explain about my using your cabin."

"That's all right," said Tom awkwardly. "It was empty. You a stranger in these parts?"

"I was," the red-haired man replied grimly, "but I'm getting acquainted." He fingered his scarred cheek. "I'm Buck Brunt, the game warden for this district."

Tom dismounted without replying. So his uninvited guest was the man who had the thankless job of bringing

29

game laws to the mountains! One mystery was solved, anyway.

"After the Black Elk, eh?" he asked noncommittally.

The warden shot him a quick look. "My job is enforcing the game laws—all of them."

Still holding the leash, Tom walked up to the porch and leaned his own rifle and rod against the railing. Smoky smelled the stranger over thoroughly. With a bloodhound's curiosity, he was investigating this new scent and filing it away in the deep mazes of his brain. Satisfied, he flopped down on the porch and paid no more attention to him.

"Look here, Tom," said the warden suddenly. "I checked up on you when I got to Hilldale yesterday. Pop Halvorsen said you'd always been a square shooter, and so had your dad. Said he was a man who observed every game law before it was ever on the books. Your dad believed in leaving something for the next man, and the next generation. So do you. I need somebody who can help me clean up this mess, somebody who knows the mountains. How about it?"

"These people in here are friends of mine. If you think I'm going to help you arrest them for shooting a little meat, you're crazy."

The warden smiled. "I'm not saying that your friends do great harm, even though they'll have to conform, too. We can educate them. But the game in this region is being systematically cleaned out by market butchers. You've heard of the Black Elk outfit already. Everybody has, but nobody will talk. I can't get him alone, partly because he's smart and it's a big region, but mostly

30

because your mountain friends are too closemouthed to give even a pirate like that away! But they know you and will talk to you."

Tom shook his head. "I told you these people are friends of mine. I reckon I'll mind my own affairs."

"You're like all the rest!" Buck Brunt said with sudden anger. "You can't see anything that doesn't lie in front of your nose! Yeah, I know that old Bill Tolliver and twenty like him have been shooting game in here since the year one! Do you think that can go on forever? There just isn't that much game. Wildlife belongs to all the people, not to a few! Someday these mountains of yours will be a wonderful recreational area for all who want to get out and see what nature is like. Neither you nor all your hard-skulled hillbilly friends can prevent it! We have the law on our side and the law will win! There are some who realize that already."

"Who?"

"This skunk who calls himself the Black Elk, for one. Why do you think he's in such a hurry to clean out the mountains now? Because he knows that he can't get away with it much longer. We'll close his markets and arrest the thoughtless people who buy the wildlife he butchers. And we'll get him, as well as the whole yellow crew that's helping him!"

Tom was impressed. The warden was hot-tempered and openly scornful, but Tom had to admire his zeal and courage. If it was only just a matter of the Black Elk, and didn't involve his friends!

"Sorry I can't see it your way," he said lamely. "It's just—"

31

"So am I," snapped Buck Brunt. "It's your choice, friend. I'll move my stuff out and be on my way."

"You needn't work up a sweat about it," Tom replied. "The cabin's big enough for two for a few days."

"I don't think your mountaineer pals would like it much," the warden sneered.

Tom flushed. "It's my cabin."

"Do you really feel that way?" the redhead asked.

"Yeah."

"Then I'll stay until I find another cabin. Thanks. Be seeing you."

Catching up his rifle, the hotheaded warden mounted his horse and rode down the trail.

Tom stared after him, half-minded to call him back. He did not like the idea of game from his mountains being sold through markets. No mountain man would conceive such a scheme, and if local men were involved it was a safe bet that they were directed by someone else, some outsider. Mountain-bred himself, Tom resented all trespassers by instinct.

As he led Pete to the corral and rubbed him down, he considered and reconsidered the warden's offer. Two men could succeed where one would fail. And success would mean breaking up a poaching ring that might otherwise strip the mountains clean. But who was involved in the ring? Some of them were sure to be mountaineers he knew—men who had always led their own lives and let others lead theirs, as he had.

"I reckon not," he finally murmured to Pete. "Guess I'll hang fire and mind my own business."

32

When he came back to the cabin, Smoky was standing on the edge of the porch, head held high. He was testing the air, apparently reading with his nose the direction Buck Brunt was taking. Few dogs of any breed could pick up body scent at the distance which the red-haired warden must have covered by now. Tom looked thoughtfully at the big hound.

"You've got a nose, all right," he said, "and I've trained a couple of hounds in my day. If I can bring you around, there won't be a cold trailer in the mountains that can touch you. Come here, Smoky."

The tawny hound's toenails clicked on the porch as he padded across to Tom. When he raised his head, Tom smiled at the perpetually sad expression. Then the smile broke. He had always cherished a theory that all good dogs considered that they owned their masters as much as they were owned by them. He thought he saw that trait already reflected in Smoky's eyes. The tawny hound regarded Tom as an equal. He felt that he had acquired a friend, and not a master. Tom reached down to scratch the floppy ears. Smoky shoved his heavy jaw against Tom's leg, and sighed contentedly.

"Even Bill Tolliver can't tell me that a hound like you won't run game," Tom said, straightening up. "Anyhow, now is a good time to find out." He picked up his rifle and the end of Smoky's leash.

The black boar's tracks were hours old, but any hound with a nose as keen as Smoky's should be able to pick them up and follow them. Not that he expected one hound to bring the big beast to bay and hold him. He merely wished to see what Smoky could do on a game trail. If he could learn to hunt game, there would be good sport in future.

Pete nickered anxiously when they passed the corral, but Tom left the black and white pinto where he was. Though Smoky had already proven his ability to run with a horse, even when he was leashed, it would be better to walk when trying to teach him how to hunt. Then he could give all his attention to the dog.

When they came to the burn on top of the mountain, Tom dropped a little behind. The tawny hound hesitated, looked around at him, and went on. Suddenly he stopped.

His head went up, and he lifted one foreleg like a pointer's as he snuffled into the wind. He made a few uncertain motions and swung clear around. Apparently he had a scent that puzzled him, and was trying to straighten it out.

Tom unwound the rope from his wrist and stepped back to the end, leaving Smoky plenty of slack. He said and did nothing. The hound had voluntarily picked up a scent. What he himself did with it would, in large measure, determine whether he had the makings of a good hunting dog, or was just another hound. To intefere with him, or to direct him unnecessarily, would take away his initiative.

Again Smoky swung around, testing every possible angle from which a scent might come. Then he looked squarely at the spot where Tom had seen the black boar. For a moment he stood perfectly still, orienting himself and making sure that this was the scent he wanted.

Then, with a slow, methodical step, he pulled forward.

Tom followed, keeping near enough to give Smoky slack rope and freedom in which to work, but staying far enough behind so that he did not interfere. He was exultant. Bill Tolliver had been wrong about the tawny hound. Smoky was not only a game hunter but, rarest of all, he was a natural hunter. He had proven it by voluntarily picking up the boar's scent. If he lived up to the promise he was showing, then Tom had a single dog which would be almost as valuable as a pack. Hounds able to find a very cold trail were nearly as rare as the proverbial hen's teeth.

A slow and deliberate dog, one that never moved until he was certain of where that move would take him, Smoky dipped his muzzle to the ground and snuffled prodigiously. Then he dropped back to verify a wisp of scent that he had picked up. With painful slowness he moved into the brush, his head still to the ground so he could keep his nose near the elusive trail he had discovered.

Tom followed happily. Many hours after it had been laid, Smoky was slowly but surely on the trail of the black boar. That alone proved the quality of both his nose and his hunting instinct. Even Twig, undisputed leader of Bill Tolliver's pack, could not find a trail this old and follow it so surely. Old Bill had missed a good bet when he had so casually given the hound to Tom.

Smoky faltered, and retraced his steps to pick up the trail where he had lost it. Tom waited patiently. The sun had certainly burned out most of the boar's scent. On this hot, dry day, on the exposed burn, worse tracking conditions could hardly be imagined. It was amazing that the hound had picked up the trail at all. Then Smoky came to the edge of the burn and started straight down a trodden footpath that led into the forest.

Tom frowned. The boar was a wild thing with all the cunning ways of its kind. It seemed inconceivable that such a creature would venture upon a trail used by man, much less follow it for any distance. Yet Smoky did not hesitate. Half reluctantly, Tom followed. The nose of a good dog was far more acute than the sharpest eyes of any human. If a hunter could not trust his hound, then he was better off without it. Now was the time to find out whether Smoky's nose could be trusted.

The dog swung away from the trail and into the brush. Tom followed, brushing aside clusters of half-ripened huckleberries as he made his way behind the big hound. His waning confidence returned. All wild animals are individualistic. The black boar, for reasons of his own, had seen fit to walk for a while on a path trodden by humans. Then he had left it for the more normal course that a wild thing would choose.

Tom followed Smoky down a sunbaked slope and into a valley dotted with clumps of aspens. He looked ahead. On the far side of the valley rose another slope, marked by a single pine that towered on its flank like a sentinel. The course Smoky was following took them up the mountain toward the tree. Tom paused to wipe the sweat from his face and went on.

Smoky broke into a little trot and Tom had to run to keep up with him. The tawny hound strained to the end

36

of the leash toward the big pine. When he reached it he leaped up the trunk.

Tom stood back, baffled by the hound's actions. The boar certainly hadn't climbed the tree. What was the matter with Smoky, anyhow? Had he picked up the body scent of a bear or wildcat? If so, he would naturally bay his treed quarry. Tom spoke sharply.

"Get down there!"

The big hound dropped back to the base of the pine and stood for an irresolute moment. Then he struck directly through the brush, toward a fringe of tall trees that hemmed it in. Tom followed, more and more puzzled as the silent hound advanced. No normal hound should act as Smoky was acting. Yet he was clearly on a trail. Tom had to believe what he saw.

Deep in the forest, Smoky stopped suddenly. He stood tense and quivering, one forepaw lifted. A low growl bubbled in his throat. Tom walked up and quieted the big hound. Just ahead was a trail, one of many that wound through the forest, and Smoky was watching it. Something must be coming down that trail!

Tom shortened the rope. Holding the hound close to him, he slipped behind a tree. From there he advanced to another, and another, until he could look down the trail. Tom stared in disbelief.

Coming down the path was a bareheaded little man with a shock of ragged brown hair that tumbled all over his head. The little man was peering ahead through thick, horn-rimmed glasses, raising his feet high and bringing them down carefully so they would make no noise. He wore a blue sports shirt, blue trousers, and soft low shoes. Obviously he was not a native. A streetcar coming down the lonely trail could not have been much more surprising than this mild little creature. Then Tom noticed the ugly black automatic he carried in his hand.

He was traveling very slowly, intent on the trail ahead. He would bend down as if looking for tracks, straighten up and peer all around, then stop to listen before going on again.

Tom let him go past, then spoke abruptly.

"You lose something, bud?"

The little man whirled so swiftly that his tumbled hair rearranged itself in an entirely new pattern. He lifted his automatic, then dropped it and laughed nervously. When he spoke, his voice was a squeaky falsetto.

"Oh dear yes! I mean oh dear no! I lost nothing!"

"For a man who hadn't lost anything, you were looking mighty hard."

"I am looking for a wild boar," the little man explained. "For a black Russian boar that roams these woods. I am Chalmers Garsoney, and I am studying the wildlife of the mountains so I may write about it. I thought that I might find signs of the boar on this trail."

"So you are a student of wild life, eh?"

"My whole career," Chalmers Garsoney said proudly, "has been devoted to studying creatures of the wild."

"And you look for a wild boar on an open trail? Did you expect to find him poking along like a porcupine?"

"It is not unreasonable to suppose that it might travel this trail."

"Well, it could be," Tom agreed. "Have you seen his tracks?"

"I came upon them in a burned area on top of the mountain. The boar must have crossed it recently."

"He did," Tom admitted. "I saw him. And he's a whacking big brute with an ugly look in his eye. He could make hash out of you in two seconds—unless you could hit him with that cannon you're carrying."

"I feel quite capable of defending myself, thank you," the little man replied stiffly.

Smoky had strained forward to snuffle Chalmers Garsoney thoroughly. Tom looked dispiritedly at the tawny hound. Old Bill had been right. Smoky was a natural-born man hunter and had no interest whatever in game. He had been on the trail of Chalmers Garsoney all the time. Now he was merely verifying the scent he had been following. Tom looked up.

"Why did you climb that big pine on top of the mountain?"

"I thought it might offer me a commanding view from which I might see the black boar."

"You must have seen us in the valley."

"I did, and naturally wondered why your dog was tracking me. Isn't he a bloodhound?"

"He's part bloodhound," Tom admitted ruefully, "but I didn't know he was tracking you. I thought he'd taken the boar's trail and was on it."

The little man laughed sympathetically. "Well, better luck next time. If you will excuse me, I shall be on with my studies."

"Go ahead. But take care of yourself. That boar is ugly."

"Thank you," the little man said. "I will be careful."

The self-styled student of wildlife went on down the trail and Tom cut back through the forest toward his cabin.

He was both amused and puzzled by Chalmers Garsoney. Of all the strange things that had invaded the mountains during his absence, the little nature lover was the most unexpected. What a way to stalk game— stepping daintily down an open trail with an automatic!

Was he the harmless crackpot he appeared to be? He had seen Tom and Smoky from the pine tree, and had assumed they were following him. Maybe he was backtracking his own trail to do a little bushwhacking!

No, that was absurd. The little man certainly wasn't much of a woodsman, but should know that he wouldn't have a chance against a mountaineer with a rifle and a dog. Tom shook his head. He had seen and heard too much since getting off the train in Hilldale. He was growing suspicious of everything and everybody.

Well, he had learned one thing: Smoky was more bloodhound than Plott hound. He had hoped that the big dog would run game. Apparently he wouldn't. Since Tom hadn't any intention of hunting men, the hound was of little practical value. He might be good company, and the cabin probably would be lonesome after Buck Brunt left. Tom shrugged. He would keep Smoky as a companion, then.

As they entered the clearing, Smoky growled softly

40

and looked toward the cabin. Paying no attention, Tom walked up on the porch. He stopped in his tracks.

Somebody had been here since he left. Smoky's growl should have given him warning of that. Tom stared at the paper that was stuck in the door, pulled it out, and read it twice.

> There's enough people around here now.
> Get out within forty-eight hours or take
> what's coming to you.

The signature was a drawing of a black elk!

Tom felt the back of his neck grow warm, and fierce anger surged like a flood through him. He was being warned to get out of the mountains or suffer the consequences, was he? He crumpled the note in his hand. He had tried to avoid trouble, but apparently the Black Elk was out to find some. Well, he could have it!

Again Smoky rumbled a warning, and turned to face the trail that led out of the clearing. Dragging the hound with him, Tom stepped inside the doorway and held his rifle ready.

A minute later Buck Brunt rode in, and stopped at the corral to turn his horse in with Pete. When he came toward the cabin, Tom was standing on the porch, holding out the note.

"Read this," he demanded.

Buck Brunt unfolded the paper and read it. He looked at Tom quizzically.

"Well?"

"Is that warden's job still open?"

"Do you know what you're getting into?"

"I know that no gang of hoodlums is going to run me out of these mountains."

"What about minding your own business?" There was a half-smile on the warden's hard face.

"This *is* my business."

Buck Brunt took a leather wallet from his pocket and extracted two papers. "Then sign these."

"What are they?"

"Your appointment. One will have to go on file at headquarters. You keep the other."

Tom signed both papers without a word.

4
Night Attack

"Now," said the warden, pocketing one of the papers, "just why *did* you take the job?"

"What do you mean?"

"You don't know me from Adam. The second time I saw you I offered you a warden's job which you turned down. Now you read a threatening note and change your mind. Do you intend to use the job as a shield, to have the law on your side if somebody comes to get you?"

For a moment Tom was silent. He hadn't thought of it that way. But the red-haired warden was nobody's fool; it *was* a possibility.

"I don't know," Tom said awkwardly.

"What don't you know?"

"Why I took the job. If this Black Elk came gunning for me I'd fight him off regardless. It's just, it's just—"

43

"Just what?"

"I've seen it before. Two of the five years I've been away I spent in Eleven Acres. Miners were murdered in the streets for what they had in their pokes. The only law was your own. Then a town marshal cleaned up the place. When I left, Eleven Acres was law-abiding; you didn't have to pack a gun. I never thought of the mountains that way before, but I do now. I don't like the idea of anyone's cleaning the game out of these mountains any better than I like to have them threaten to run me out!"

"If you intend to hide behind the law, you're making a mistake," the warden warned him. "Someday a game warden may command respect in these parts. Now he's regarded as a bushwhacker who hopes to ambush innocent violators. The courts and justices are as much with the violator, and sometimes more, than they are with the warden. If, in the performance of your duty, you killed a violator, unless you had unimpeachable proof that you did it in self defense, you'd be tried for murder."

"I'm not aiming to kill anybody."

"No, but you'll have to *be* the law, and act as circumstances dictate. What are you going to do the first time you catch one of your friends violating the law you are supposed to enforce?"

"I don't know," Tom admitted frankly. "I'll have to wait and see."

Buck Brunt looked at him steadily. "All right, I'll leave it at that. We've got more important things to do than check up on everybody's Sunday dinner."

"Just what do you know about this Black Elk outfit?"

"Not much," the warden said ruefully. "There's a

44

crew of hunters out all the time, and they don't care how they get their game. They jacklight, trap, net, and I wouldn't put it past them to poison. They also buy as much as they can, I suspect. They net and dynamite fish, especially trout. The only two things I'm sure of is that the brains behind the whole affair are plenty smart, and that Fred Larsen does most of their packing."

"How do you know that?"

"He's the only one with enough horses to do it."

"Why don't you catch him?"

"I want to find out who's working with him. There are a lot of people in these mountains."

"Say, did you ever run across a little man named Chalmers Garsoney?"

"Yeah. Harmless little nut. He stays at the Hilldale Hotel and spends most of his time pussyfooting around the trails. Going to write a book, he says. You seen him?"

"Saw him today," Tom laughed. "Maybe you should hire him, too."

"He might be useful, at that," Buck answered soberly. "We'll need all the help we can get, and I've got some. There's a fellow named Johnny Magruder coming in tomorrow. He was crazy enough to take a warden's job, too. Good man, though."

Tom looked at the warden, and grinned. "Well, there's nothing more to worry about. They're coming to get me within forty-eight hours, and I'll clean out the whole works for you."

"Yeah? This is no joke, sonny boy. I aim to be right around here when they come, and I'll have Johnny here if he gets in in time. They won't be coming by daylight; it'll be either tonight or tomorrow night. If they should hurt anybody they'll want to slip away without being seen."

"Don't they know they'll have the sheriff on their trail?"

"The sheriff of this county," Buck Brunt snorted, "is about as useful as bells on a buggy whip. He couldn't catch a one-legged horse if it was hog-tied. Besides, he looks on me with more suspicion than he does these poachers." He thought a moment. "I'm going to ride into Hilldale and send a wire to Johnny Magruder. I'll tell him to come directly to your cabin instead of to Hilldale; he can get off at Martinton and hike over the Klesa Trail. It might be fun to have three men around when the Black Elk comes to run you out."

"It might at that."

The warden went down to the corral for his horse. He stopped on the way back.

"Stick tight to the cabin," he called. "I'll be back tonight. Anything you want?"

"Bring me a box of 30-30s when you come, and a load of grub. Tell Pop Halvorsen to put it on my bill."

"*Our* bill," the warden corrected him. "So long."

When Buck had gone, Tom stood still, a little amazed at what he had done. He had acted partly on angry impulse when he had accepted Buck Brunt's offer of a warden's job. But it was still a fact that if something was not done about it, there would be nothing in the mountains for Bill Tolliver, Wayne McCloud, Hank Jamieson, or anyone else, to hunt. Tom thought of his father. Like

46

all the rest, Carver Rainse had taken most of his living from the mountains. But he had been a fair hunter. He had never taken more than he could use, and he had never hunted or fished one place until it was depleted of wildlife. There must always be something left.

Tom tickled Smoky's ears. "How do you like that?" he said to the big hound. "Home one day and I've got a new horse, a new dog, and a new job! Well, time for supper."

He carried his rifle into the cabin and exchanged it for his fishing rod. It was a split bamboo which he himself had made. He jointed it up and tested the action. Light as a feather but strong as steel, the rod seemed a live thing in his hands. A smile of sheer satisfaction lighted his face. Fishing was unsurpassed sport when correctly done with the right equipment.

He clamped a reel to the rod, strung a line through the guides, attached a gossamer leader, and tied a single fly to it. Smoky padded behind him as he walked cautiously down to the creek, whipped the rod to get line, and cast. The fly alighted perfectly, floated a second, and then there was a gentle ripple as it was sucked under. Tom struck. The wandlike rod bent almost double as the fish on the other end fought back savagely. Tom let him tire, then played him into the bank and lifted him out. For a second he admired his catch, a two-and-a-half-pound rainbow. Then he looked regretfully at the creek and turned away. It would be fun to fish some more, but the trout he had would more than make a meal for himself and Smoky. To take any more would be a pointless waste of wildlife. Besides, he told himself with a chuckle, he was a game warden now.

Twilight had fallen by the time Tom had cooked the trout and shared it with Smoky. Leaving the dishes where they were, he grasped one end of the table and dragged it across the floor to a position in front of the window. He pulled a chair up to the table, and arranged a lamp so that its reflected light would fall squarely across the chair.

Then he rummaged in the closet for an old shirt, and came upon the blue denim Buck Brunt had been wearing the first time he saw him. Grinning broadly to himself, Tom stuffed it full of rags. Buttoning the shirt around its filling, he propped it up in the chair. For a moment he stood back to inspect his handiwork. It was all right as far as it went, but . . .

"Come on, Smoky," he said, "I've got an idea."

Smoky followed him outside, and Pete nickered a greeting. Tom remembered that he had seen an abandoned wasp nest dangling from one of the willows along the creek. The wasps had no further use for it, but he did. He groped in the darkness until he had located the nest, cut the branch that held it, and carried it into the cabin. He set it carefully on top of the shirt, moved the lamp a little, and stepped outside to look. He walked inside to turn the lamp a bit lower and went out to look again.

The shirt and wasp nest did not look exactly like a man bending over a table, but maybe it would do. Whoever came to get him would be nervous and not too disposed to examine anything closely—if they intended to come shooting. Tom left the lamp burning. With Smoky be-

48

side him and the rifle across his lap, he waited on a dark corner of the porch.

A pale star blinked, then another, and suddenly a million seemed to bloom all over the sky. An hour passed.

Suddenly Smoky raised his head, growled, and stood up. Tom pushed him down. The tawny hound tensed himself and again got up, the soft growl rumbling in his throat. He was looking toward the trail.

Tom slipped from the porch, crouched in the cabin's shadow, and pressed Smoky to the ground. This time the dog remained. He had learned in only two lessons that, when Tom pushed him down, he was supposed to stay there.

Quietly, making no swift moves that would attract attention, Tom swung the rifle around and cocked it. Smoky remained silent, centering all his attention on whoever was coming up the trail. A dim figure broke out of the trees and into the clearing. Tom let him come. When the approaching man was less than ten yards away, Tom challenged him sharply.

"Stop right there!"

The figure halted. There was a moment's silence that was broken by a low laugh and Buck Brunt's voice.

"Take it easy, Tom. I'm saving my money for my old age!"

Tom clicked his rifle back to safe and walked out to meet the warden. He was carrying a pack on his shoulders. Buck's teeth showed white as he laughed again.

"How'd you know I was coming?"

"Smoky knew it two minutes before you got here. That hound's got a real nose. I'm beginning to depend on what he says."

"Well, if you've got a dog like that it's a sure thing that nobody's going to bushwhack you."

"That's all right with me. What'd you do with your horse?"

"I tied him back in the brush. If these birds come tonight it may be just as well if they think there's only one person to meet 'em."

"There's been no sign of them yet."

"Don't be so anxious; the night's young. Here's your 30-30s. I've got a load of grub for you, too."

"Bring it in."

Tom led the way into the cabin and turned up the lamp on the table. Buck Brunt deposited his pack on an empty chair, straightened, and looked with amusement at Tom's creation.

"Who's that supposed to be?"

"Me, of course. If I didn't have bees in my bonnet I never would have taken this job."

"Hey, isn't that my shirt?" the warden demanded.

"Sure. I don't want any holes shot in mine."

"Do you think it'll fool 'em?" Buck laughed.

"It depends on how far away they are. Come on out and see."

Tom turned the lamp down and they went outside. The warden looked through the window, chuckling.

"It might do the trick at that. What's your plan, mastermind?"

"To let them make the first move. I don't hanker to be in the cabin at night if this Black Elk's really serious. I'll be out here where I can move around."

"That's smart enough. Looks like about all we can do now is wait."

Side by side, with Smoky crouched between them, they waited in the cabin's shadow. As the night wore on, Tom crawled into the cabin to blow the lamp out. Everything had to appear natural, if the raiders were to be lured into revealing themselves. Maybe they were waiting for the light to go out, anyway.

"Might as well sleep," Buck whispered. "It takes only one to watch. I'll catch an hour, then you take an hour."

"All right."

The warden slid down on the grass, pillowed his head on his arms, and immediately went to sleep. Smoky was already dozing beside Tom. Out in the forest an owl hooted. A little later a fox barked. Tom nodded, and jerked himself erect. He looked at the silver moon that had risen among the stars. Buck had slept for more than an hour. Tom reached over to prod him in the ribs. The warden came instantly awake, but lay quietly until he knew exactly what was going on.

"You take it a while," Tom whispered. "I'm getting sleepy."

"All right."

"Watch Smoky. He'll let you know if anything comes."

Tom lay down in the grass, pillowed his head on his hands, and fell asleep. He would awaken in an hour, he

51

assured himself, and let the warden sleep. There needn't be anything to worry about; Smoky would certainly give plenty of warning . . .

Tom sat hastily erect and reached for his rifle, knowing that the Black Elk had come upon them unawares. In some way he had managed to set the cabin on fire. Its heat was stealing over him, threatening to roast him alive.

He rubbed his eyes, and found himself bathed in the warm rays of the early morning sun. Smoky still remained beside him, but Buck Brunt was gone. Then Tom became aware of the delicious aroma of frying bacon, and fresh coffee. The red-haired warden came out on the porch.

"You going to sleep all day?"

"Why didn't you wake me up?"

"You looked so nice and peaceful I just didn't have the heart. Besides, I got interested in watching your flop-eared dog. That hound's going to be all right."

"Did you hear or see anything?"

"Couple of deer and a bull elk that galloped across the clearing. Nothing else. Come on in and eat."

Tom picked up his rifle, entered the cabin, and sat down to the great stack of pancakes and platter of fried bacon that Buck had prepared. He ate until he could eat no more, then pushed his chair back and fed the remaining pancakes to Smoky, one by one.

"One night and no score," the warden said thoughtfully. "Unless this Black Elk aims to make a liar out of himself he'll sure come tonight."

"What about today?"

"He won't come in the daylight. He's got more sense."

"I'll still stick around."

"Then I'll ride to Martinton and pick up Johnny Magruder. I'm not sure he knows the Klesa Trail, and I don't want him going astray. Johnny always did like fireworks, and he'd never speak to me again if I let him miss those that are likely to be going off around here tonight."

"Beat it, then. I'll clean up."

Buck Brunt buckled his gun belt on and started down the trail after his horse. Tom poured hot water out of the blackened tea kettle, washed the dishes, and cleaned the cabin. As soon as the table was clear he laid his rifle and a handful of cartridges on it. He was jumpy; nothing could be more nerve-racking than waiting around for something that might or might not happen. Then he looked at Smoky and was reassured.

The tawny hound lay on the porch, dozing in the early-morning sun. He slept peacefully, but there was still a part of him that never slept. Smoky's nose was always awake. Not once had he failed to give warning when a stranger approached. He might not be much of a game hound, but it was mighty comforting to have him around.

Pete nickered a cheerful greeting when Tom went out to the corral, and came up to the fence to nuzzle his hand when he opened the gate. Tom slipped a bridle on the black and white pinto, attached a thirty-foot tie rope, and led Pete out of the corral. In two days the horse had eaten much of the grass and trampled the rest, but there was plenty more in the clearing. Tom staked Pete in the center of a lush patch and left the tough little horse contentedly grazing while he busied himself about the cabin. A dozen times he glanced nervously out of the window.

Then he saw Smoky standing on the edge of the porch. The sad-faced hound was gazing at the end of the clearing. He did not growl, but looked back at the cabin as though wondering where Tom might be. Tom picked up his rifle and slipped around the corner of the cabin. He waited tensely, reading Smoky as Smoky read the wind.

A minute later old Bill Tolliver rode into the clearing, leading a brown pack horse.

Tom quietly entered the cabin, left his rifle on the table, and went out to meet Bill. The old man's eyes were clouded and angry. His beard worked spasmodically as he clenched and unclenched his jaws.

"Hello, Tawm," he growled.

"Hi, Bill. What rubbed you the wrong way?"

"Plenty. When I came across the burn I found somethin' that plumb tore me up! Three cow elk and three calves tried to cross it, they did, and somebody got all six! I could almost understand the sense in a game warden if he ketched such killers!"

"Maybe he'd like to."

"Mebbe nothin'! He's afraid to go after 'em, that's what he is!"

Tom said nothing. Tolliver did not yet know that he was a game warden, and perhaps that was just as well. The old man's sense of loyalty was strong, but still stronger was his hatred of anything that restricted the freedom he had enjoyed all his life. The showdown with old Bill Tolliver could come later, if it had to come at all.

"I fetched the rest of your gear over, Tawm," the old man said. "There's your shotguns, twenty-two, the rest of your fishin' tackle, and such-like. Mother Tolliver sent a whackin' big mess of grub—even roasted a ha'nch of venison for you. Said you got no business livin' alone, without some woman to at least help look out for you."

"A haunch of venison?"

"Sure. What's the matter? Thought you liked venison?"

"I do, Bill. Much obliged. And thanks for toting all my stuff over."

He should, he supposed, arrest Bill Tolliver now. Only he couldn't. Bill hadn't the faintest idea that Tom was a warden. He was only being neighborly.

"Come in a while," Tom invited.

"Can't," the old man replied gruffly. "Got to be gettin' back. I'll leave the gear with you and you can fetch the tarp back when you happen to drop over."

He unlaced the diamond hitch that bound the pack on the horse, and carried the heavy load up on the porch. Then mounting his white horse, with the now burdenless pack horse trotting behind, he rode back up the trail.

As Tom took the various articles out of the pack and stowed them in their proper places, he suddenly remembered that Bill hadn't asked if he had discovered who was living in his cabin. A good thing! Evidently the old man had been too worked up over the slaughter of the elk to think of it.

When noon came Tom sliced off cold venison, smiling

ironically while he ate. Of all the people who should not be enjoying illegal game, certainly a game warden came first! Still, he reflected, when it came to roasting a haunch of venison, Mrs. Tolliver stood supreme.

The afternoon dragged on and at last evening shadows began to lengthen. Again Tom put his dummy in place, lighted the lamp and sought the dark corner of the porch. Smoky dozed beside him.

Tom was uneasy. Buck Brunt had promised to return with Johnny Magruder. They should be here, but as yet there had been no sign of them.

Then the big hound awakened and sat up. The short hairs on his neck bristled as he stared steadily across the clearing. Tom tensed himself. Buck and Magruder would have to come by one trail or the other; but Smoky was staring into the forest *across* the clearing. He strained his ears but could not hear a sound except a barred owl, far off. He put a quieting hand on the dog, and waited.

Out among the trees, a flame bloomed briefly, and the silence was shattered by the blast of a rifle. Tom heard the tinkle of broken glass, and knew that the bullet had gone through the window. He stood up softly, and Smoky crowded close beside him as he started across the clearing. Raising and lowering his feet carefully, making no sound, Tom advanced toward the place from which the hidden marksman had shot. He stopped in his tracks.

To his left, something moved out of the forest and into the clearing. When it stepped out of the trees, Tom saw the indistinct figure of a man outlined against the night sky. The figure drifted slowly toward the trail at the upper end of the clearing. Tom skulked after it, then broke into a silent run. Just as the man heard him and started to turn, Tom punched the muzzle of his rifle into the other's back.

"Don't try anything," he said clearly. "This rifle's loaded, too."

The man stood stock still. Tom could feel the fear that trembled through him.

"Don't you know me, Tom?" the stranger said hesitantly.

"Who?"

"Me," the voice quavered. "Hank Jamieson."

5

The Black Boar

Tom stood still, making no attempt to remove his rifle from the small of the other's back. He knew Hank Jamieson, and had always thought of him as a harmless, shiftless kind of fellow. But somebody had certainly shot through the cabin window at the dummy Tom had set up, and there was no one else around.

"What are you doing here?" he snapped.

"Not what you think, Tom."

"How do you know what I think?"

"You think I fired that shot through the window. I didn't—I swear I didn't."

"Who did?"

"I don't know." Hank Jamieson's voice became suddenly fierce. "All I know is that I followed a man over here, hopin' to get a shot at him! Night before last, that

58

Black Elk tried to burn my cabin when my woman and kids was in it! It was only by luck alone I got 'em out, but when I did I saw two of the gang that did it. I marked 'em, and I swore I'd get 'em if I could! Then, just about dark tonight, I saw one of 'em cut over the mountain thisaway. I hadn't any notion of where he was goin', but I followed him."

In the darkness, Smoky was smelling the prisoner over. It was another scent for the hound's index, something he would never forget. For a moment the only sound was his heavy snuffling as he made his inspection.

"Turn around, Hank," Tom ordered, "and go back to the cabin. I'll follow you."

"All right, Tom."

Hank Jamieson swung around and started toward the cabin. Careful to stay close behind him, and to keep his rifle ready, Tom followed him up on the porch.

"Open the door, Hank."

As they walked into the cabin, Smoky crowded close behind them, and lay down in his customary place in front of the stove. Tom glanced at the dummy that had been in front of the shattered window. The dry wasp nest lay in tattered shreds on top of the shirt and over the table. Tom felt a cold chill. A dumdum bullet had been used. Had a man been sitting in place of the dummy, he would never again trouble the Black Elk.

"Lay your rifle on the table, Hank," he ordered.

As his prisoner obeyed, Tom looked him over. Hank was tall and angular, like most mountaineers, and a little more stooped than Tom had remembered him. There was a slight hint of a paunch, too, which most mountain men lacked. Hank, Tom recalled, had never been noted for a desire to work hard, or even work at all if he could help it. He had always been one to sleep and loaf when he wasn't hunting or fishing.

Tom pointed at the dummy. "Take a look, Hank. My head would be a nice sight if it had been where that wasp nest was, wouldn't it?"

"You're right, Tom. You're dead right, but I didn't fire that shot. Let me do some talkin', will you?"

"Talk."

"Look, Tom, I always 'bided in these mountains and I always minded my own business. You know that. I never set a hand to anybody else's stuff, and never wanted to. Like everybody else I got along, and there was enough for everybody. Some time back we heard there was goin' to be a change. Game laws, they said. We couldn't hunt like we used to. That made me kind of mad, same as it did everybody else.

"Then this here Black Elk hit the country. I still tried to mind my own affairs; I figured I wouldn't pester him as long as he left me alone. Then I went out one day to get me a deer, and couldn't find any. I did find where mebbe a dozen had been killed, and that made me think. Somebody was killin' 'em off too fast. Us mountain men would be put to it to eat decent if that didn't stop. When the game warden come in and said he aimed to stop it, it seemed like a right good idea. I allowed I'd work with him, and told him to watch the lick on Haystack Mountain. Three nights later I woke up in the middle of the night to find my cabin on fire. Somebody had doused it with kerosene and throwed a match into it."

Tom said brusquely, "Go on."

"Well, I saw two of the men that set that fire," Hank Jamieson continued. "Looked through the window and saw 'em, and to my dyin' day I won't forget 'em. One was taller than I be, big, and with curly black hair. The other was smaller. I never saw either one before. But when big Black-Hair passed up Lynx Crick tonight, just about dark, I was fishin' there. I marked the trail he took, then got my rifle and followed. I aimed to kill him and I still aim to. He fired through your window. I swear he did."

"If you want to get him so bad, why were you in such a rush to get away?"

"I thought he'd killed the warden and I didn't aim to get messed up in that. I don't want no state men after me."

"The warden?"

"That's right. I didn't know you'd come back. The warden's been usin' your cabin as an overnight stop."

"So you decided to make tracks?"

"Sure. I'll get another chance."

Tom bit his lower lip. His prisoner was probably telling the truth. Hank Jamieson never had been famous for thinking of anyone except himself, and he had certainly been acting in character. When he thought that Buck Brunt might lie badly hurt in the cabin, he had run away to avoid risk to himself. But Tom was not satisfied.

"If you followed this man from Lynx Creek," he persisted, "why is it that you didn't get a shot at him before he got here?"

"Like I said, I had to go home and get my rifle, and all

61

I saw was the trail he took. I followed it, and got here just in time to catch the flash of his rifle when he shot. Thought I'd have one look for him and scoot if I couldn't find him quick."

Smoky growled, walked to the door, and scratched to go out. Tom looked at him, and started to back toward the door, still keeping his eyes on his prisoner. He was certain of just two things: a shot had been fired through the cabin window, and he had caught a man in the clearing. He was taking no chances that the two facts were not directly connected.

He ducked almost instinctively; he had seen another red flash out among the trees. As he threw himself down he felt the bullet whistle close to his head.

Hank Jamieson snatched his rifle from the table and crouched beside Tom.

"I told you," the mountain man breathed. "He's come back."

Tom crawled to the table, reached cautiously up with his free hand, slid the lamp off, and blew it out. He crept to the door and pushed Smoky aside while he edged it open.

"What d'you aim to do?" Hank whispered.

"Go out and get him."

Tom quietly pushed the door open and crawled through onto the porch. He inched across to the shaded corner, and stood up. Hank Jamieson joined him silently. Smoky's nails clicked as the big hound padded up beside them. In the darkness, Tom reached down to quiet him. The dog was alert, every muscle tense, as he pointed his nose toward the forest.

"Walk beside me, Hank," Tom whispered. "We'll follow the dog."

"I'm with you."

Smoky started off across the clearing, angling toward the forest. The two men followed him, Hank moving a little ways away. That was a smart move. If whoever had fired the shot intended to shoot again he would have to pick his target. Then, even if he shot straight, the man he did not hit could return his fire. Tom remained still until Hank Jamieson started walking, then moved slowly ahead, one hand on the dog.

Smoky paced beside Tom, his head in the air and snuffling audibly as he walked toward the trees. They came to a stump at the edge of the clearing and the hound thrust his nose to the earth while he drank deeply of what was apparently a hot scent. At a whispered word from Tom, he began to snuffle along the ground, straight into the forest. Five minutes later Tom stopped. Their man evidently hadn't paused.

"He shot from behind the stump all right," Tom told Hank, "but he's gone now. We can't trail him in the dark. Come on back to the cabin."

Side by side the two walked back to the dark cabin. Tom lighted the lamp, but was careful to keep away from the window. Smoky threw himself down beside the stove again and dozed. Tom looked at him gratefully. Smoky had given warning that a stranger was near, and would again.

Hank shifted his feet nervously.

"If you don't mind, Tom, reckon I'll be gettin' along. I'm sorry I brought any trouble onto you. I figured this was my fight, and I don't want nobody else hurt."

"That's all right, Hank. It's my fight, too. Go on home if you want to, or you can bunk here tonight."

"Thanks, Tom, but I'll jolt along. Say, don't tell nobody I was here, will you? I—I wouldn't want to get burnt out again."

"If you say so. So long."

After Hank left, Tom turned the lamp lower, took a blanket outside, and curled up in the dabin's dark corner, Smoky beside him. For a long while he lay awake. Obviously something had gone wrong. Buck Brunt had promised to be back with Magruder. Maybe they'd missed connections or had run into something which the red-haired warden considered more important. Tom dozed.

He awoke with a start to see the sky glowing with the first dim light of early dawn. Smoky got to his feet, stretched, and looked around. For a moment Tom watched the big hound, then got up himself. The clearing was quiet and peaceful, with no sign of life except Pete, who had already begun to crop the dewy grass. Tom made a mental note to have Pop Halvorsen haul out some oats for the lithe little horse. He hadn't needed any as yet because he had not been worked hard. But if Smoky turned out to be the dog Tom thought he was, Pete's hard work was due to begin this morning.

Whoever fired through the cabin window last night had certainly left a trail. The scent would be only hours old, and Smoky's bloodhound nose could follow such a trail easily. Tom had heard of bloodhounds following a trail four days old.

"It'll be you and Pete and me," Tom told him as they entered the cabin. "You seem to like man-scent better than a game trail, and here's your chance."

Smoky wagged an amiable tail, but looked as mournful as ever as he lay down near the table. Tom cooked and ate a hearty breakfast. Then he got his rifle and the fifteen-foot lead rope Bill Tolliver had given him to bring Smoky home, and tied one end around the dog's neck. He didn't want the big hound to be overcome by excitement and take off on the trail by himself.

Tom mounted, and walked Pete to the stump behind which the unseen rifleman had crouched last night. Smoky strained to the end of the rope, snuffling eagerly as he worked his pendulous jowls. He halted at the stump and again inhaled the scent that arose from it. Tom rode a little nearer, slackening the rope and giving Smoky room. Some dogs needed encouragement and training, and some were natural-born hunters that just couldn't be kept from tracking their quarry. Smoky certainly acted like the latter.

Well fed and rested, Pete was impatient to be off. But Tom sat silently in the saddle. Smoky was not a trained man hunter, although he had exhibited a great interest in every man he met, and had voluntarily taken Garsoney's trail instead of the boar's. But to say or do the wrong thing now could discourage him. A trailing dog had to work out a scent in the way best suited to him.

After a moment's investigation, Smoky strained to the end of the rope and started off in the same direction he had taken during the night. This time, Tom thought grimly, he was on the right trail. It led right up the mountain. Fortunately the forest was open here, so Pete had little difficulty in following the hound. Even so, Tom was kept busy keeping Pete far enough behind so he would not interfere, but near enough to give Smoky slack. Several times he had to duck as they went under low branches, and twice the rope snagged on brush.

They came to the top of the mountain and out on a beaten trail. Not traveling fast, but keeping a steady pace, Smoky started down the path. Tom urged Pete into a little trot. This was the Klesa Trail, which wound across the mountains to Martinton. If whoever had laid the scent Smoky was following had gone clear to Martinton, it would be very difficult to ferret him out of the twelve hundred people in the little backwoods metropolis. He could still try, Tom told himself, and if he did . . . He tightened his jaw. If he ever found the person who had tried to kill him last night, somebody was going to be sorry!

The trail dipped, climbed another mountain, and dipped again. Smoky stopped suddenly, holding his head high and snuffling. He swerved so that he stood at an angle, while he fixed his eyes on a patch of laurel about five hundred yards ahead. When he continued, his head was up instead of down. He halted again and the familiar bubbling growl rumbled in his throat.

Tom slid off the pinto, dropped the reins over the little horse's head, and looped Smoky's rope about his hand. He tugged gently, and the big hound came back to him. Tom raised his rifle, balancing the muzzle across his left hand. Somebody was in or near that patch of laurel, and Tom was out in the open.

He stepped quietly off the trail and into the forest, so there would be trees between himself and the laurel. Keeping Smoky on a short lead, he advanced slowly. He reached the last tree, a grey-boled beech, and stopped behind it.

The laurel was scarcely thirty feet ahead. It was thick, heavy stuff with stalks that varied from the diameter of a lead pencil to the thickness of a man's arm. Its dense growth and shiny green leaves effectively concealed anything that might be behind them. A stray breeze rippled the leaves, and Tom stared intently.

Laurel leaves should be green, but when they blew apart he had seen a splash of bright red. There was blood on those leaves. Something, or somebody, had been hurt there.

Tom and Smoky walked slowly forward, keeping their eyes on the laurel patch. If anyone lay in ambush there the advantage now belonged to him. He could shoot from concealment. But, unless his rifle or revolver were already trained, he would have to make some move before he shot.

When he stepped from behind the sheltering tree, Tom staked everything on detecting that move. Nothing appeared. He advanced slowly, a step at a time, alert for the slightest movement.

There was none. Tom reached the thicket and, with Smoky pressing close beside him, parted the outermost branches with the muzzle of his rifle. Tom suppressed a gasp.

The thicket was not solid. It was merely a fringe of laurel that had grown about a damp mud wallow. On the damp, rotten leaves that had filtered into the wallow, a man was lying face down. He was covered with mud and blood. All about, deeply imprinted in the moist earth, were tracks of the wild boar. A tall man, Hank Jamieson had said, with black hair . . . Tom looked at the man, and back at the boar tracks in the mud. Swiftly he went forward.

He knelt beside the wounded man, and noted the irregular rise and fall of his chest. He was still alive, but cruelly cut by the black boar's razor-sharp fangs. Flowing blood had soaked his clothing. Tom looked at the shredded laurel stalks around the wallow. There had been a furious battle here, no question of it, and the man who so accurately fitted Hank Jamieson's description of the hidden bushwhacker had had the worst of it. Tom looked around for a rifle. There was no evidence of any sort of weapon.

The fallen man opened his eyes, stared unseeingly at Tom, and closed them again. Tom took his handkerchief, dipped it in the cold wetness of the wallow, and wiped the other's face. The wounded man opened his eyes again, and this time faint recognition showed in them. Tom spoke swiftly.

"I've got a horse down there and I'm going to take you to it. See if you can help."

As gently as possible, Tom half carried, half dragged the injured man away from the wallow and onto higher ground. Then he ran back for Pete. He had found his bushwhacker, but not in the way he had expected. This man was badly hurt, in urgent need of help, and because he was a human being he deserved it.

When Tom returned, the injured man stirred feebly. Tom bent close to his ear.

"Can you hear me?"

"Yes," the other whispered.

"I have a horse on the trail. I'm going to put you on him and take you to Tolliver's. It isn't far."

"All right."

Tom passed a hand around the man's shoulders and head, and the wounded man laid a weak arm across Tom's shoulders. As gently as he could, Tom lifted him to his feet. The man was severely injured, but there was nothing wrong with his courage. He made a valiant attempt to use his own legs and supported himself as much as he could. Tom guided him out of the laurel and into the trail.

Pete looked around, mildly surprised, and rolled an interested eye while Tom lifted one of the wounded man's feet into a stirrup. The man grasped the horn to pull himself into the saddle as Tom lifted. As soon as he was seated, his head drooped. He sagged and almost fell forward. Tom looked gratefully at the pinto, who was standing like a rock. The little horse seemed to sense that this was no time to balk.

"All right, Pete," Tom said, steadying the rider. "Easy does it."

Walking very gently, the pinto started down the trail. He chose his own way, avoiding all rough travel, until Tom directed him to the branch trail that led to the Tolliver clearing. When the hounds began to bay, old Bill Tolliver appeared in his doorway.

"What in tarnation?"

"The black boar's finally got his man, Bill. I brought him here because your place was the nearest. He's in bad shape."

"Well, don't stand there! Let's get him in."

The injured man collapsed in their arms as they helped ease him down. They carried him into the cabin and laid him on a bed. Bill took one look at the man's ugly gashes and turned to Elaine.

"Ride to Hilldale for the doctor. This man's hurt bad."

"Let me go," Tom protested.

"You're stayin' here," Bill grunted. "Mother will take care of him, and Elaine's as good as a man on a horse." He reached down a rifle from the gun rack. "You and me will pick up Joab Lane, and mebbe Lead Dather and Hank Jamieson. This time we're goin' to get that Black Devil!"

6

The Hunt

As Tom followed Bill Tolliver down to the corral, he saw Elaine riding away from the clearing on a spirited little sorrel mare. She could ride, he noted with approval, and seemed to know how to get the most out of her mount.

Tom had quite a few things to take up with the man wounded by the boar, but obviously he could not do it now. The black-haired man was not going anywhere for a long while, and Tom might better forget him and go along on the hunt. He knew where it should start. Furthermore, they'd need all the men they could get if they should run down the boar. Having spilled a man's blood once, the ugly beast knew perfectly well that he was capable of doing it again, and because of it was sure to be doubly dangerous.

Bill strode to the corral, picked up a lasso, and flung a loop that settled neatly over the white neck of his iron-jawed, evil-tempered saddle horse. Without ceremony he drew the squealing, fighting beast to him and snubbed the rope on a post. Expertly avoiding flying heels and bared teeth, Bill bridled and saddled his charger and mounted. He slid his rifle into the saddle scabbard and looked impatiently around.

"You ready?" he barked.

"All set," Tom replied, swinging up on Pete.

Smoky waited expectantly, panting a little in the heat. Bill's hounds trotted hopefully around and around their master. Usually, when Bill rode, a hunt impended. Other times he rode without the hounds, but always let the pack know if he wanted company.

"Hi-eee! Bring 'em along, Twig!" yelled the old man. He dug his heels into the flanks of his white horse, and the mount sprang away.

The hounds joyfully strung out behind their master, while Tom and Smoky brought up the rear. Bill Tolliver had always boasted that if he didn't have the fastest horse in the mountains, he'd get another. The white stallion was a fractious beast, but Tom had to admit that he could travel. However, Pete was having no difficulty in keeping up, and Smoky loped easily along beside the pinto. The big hound certainly was not a pack dog; he refused to go near the excited mob that trailed old Bill's horse.

They raced down the valley, entered a thick woods through which the pack ran single file, and burst out into another clearing. From the far end rose the mournful baying of Joab Lane's two hounds. Bill's pack gathered around Twig. When there was nothing more interesting to do they would fight savagely among themselves, but they always presented a united front to strangers.

Joab's hounds, lean and rangy trailing brutes that were noted for their fighting ability, snarled forward, only to swerve aside at the last minute. They wanted no battle with old Bill's entire pack. Then the bigger of Joab's two hounds noticed Smoky off by himself, and leaped straight at him.

The black and white hound was an inch taller at the shoulder and longer in body, but he lacked Smoky's solid compactness. His intention was to knock the tawny hound down by his rush, and then slash with his fangs. But when they came together Smoky scarcely moved; it was the black and white dog that went down.

With deceptive slowness Smoky moved in. He slashed, and blood bubbled down his challenger's shoulder. The black and white hound circled warily, sizing up his opponent, looking for weak points. But Smoky was a dog with his own style of doing everything. When the other hound attacked again, Smoky met him squarely. He closed his jaws on the side of the other's neck and began to grind them happily.

"Hi-ya! Cut that!"

A rifle in his hand, Joab Lane ran from the cabin. At the same time, Tom dismounted and raced forward. He grabbed Smoky's jaws and tried to pry them apart.

"Do somethin'!" Joab yelled. "Do somethin'! He'll kill my hound!"

"I'm trying!" Tom panted. "Come on, Smoky, blast your hide, let go!"

The big hound obediently released his enemy. As soon as he did, Joab pulled back his own dog, who strove gamely to return to the fight.

"Keep that critter on a leash, Tawm!" Bill Tolliver roared. "We can't have any more fights here! One dog's crippled a'ready." He turned to Joab. "Bring your other hound and come on. It's the Black Devil we're after; he's half killed a man."

Joab shut his injured dog in the barn and joined them with the remaining hound. As they left the clearing, Tom dug his heels into Pete's side and urged him up beside Tolliver's horse.

"Better follow me from here, Bill," he called. "I know the exact place."

"All right, but keep movin'. That trail's gettin' colder by the minute."

Tom brushed his heels across Pete's sides and the little black and white pinto leveled out to run. Smoky kept his place beside him, big ears flapping as he loped along. Tom realized that the big hound's appearance was deceptive. His legs seemed short, but he was so long-winded that he could run with the best when necessary.

When they reached the patch of laurel, Tom reined Pete to a halt and looked back. Bill Tolliver was thirty yards or more behind him, and Joab clear out of sight. As Bill fought his white horse to a stop, he looked enviously at Tom's mount.

"Want to sell that pinto?"

"Nothing doing, Bill, I like him, too."

Bill said disappointedly, "Doggone! The only horse in the mountains as can outrun mine, he is. Is this the place?"

"This is it. There's a wallow hidden by that laurel. Come on."

Joab came up and the three of them entered the laurel, while the well-trained hounds sat expectantly down to await orders. Bill and Joab bent down to examine the tracks in the soft wallow.

"What d'you make of it, Joab?" Bill asked.

"I've tracked that boar often enough so's I'd ought to know his tracks when I see 'em."

"Me too. But I wish I could get a good sight of 'em where they ain't covered by forty others. I never seen such a mess."

"Well, let's get the dogs on 'em. Call Twig in."

Old Bill whistled and Twig came through the laurel. The old hound snuffled about the wallow. She crossed and recrossed it, and sniffed about the laurel that hemmed it in. Puzzled, she sat down and looked around at her master. The old man scratched his head and spoke plaintively to the hound.

"Doggone your picter! That scent can't be too old for you to catch. Try again, Twig."

Dutifully the hound lowered her nose to the damp ground and again quartered back and forth. She made a tentative dash into the laurel, then came back.

"Get Jerry in to help her," Joab Lane suggested.

Bill called Jerry, and the second hound cast about with Twig as both sought to pick up the boar's scent. Tom frowned. The black-haired man had left his cabin last

75

night, therefore the boar's scent should be only a few hours old at most. Hounds as good as Bill's should be able to work it out.

Apparently they could not. For another ten minutes Twig and Jerry cast aimlessly back and forth, and then came back to sit apologetically at their master's feet. Bill Tolliver's face reflected astonishment.

"Can't figure it," he announced. "Twig and Jerry between 'em should pick up that scent. Both of 'em's run that boar half a dozen times, they have. Somethin's wrong."

"But what?" Tom asked. "The ground's damp, and there's plenty of tracks."

"I dunno. Mebbe the weather or somethin'. I sure can't make it out. Want to try Smoky?"

Tom shook his head. "He'd only backtrack the man. I tried to put him on the boar's trail before, and he wouldn't take it. He's a man hunter."

Old Bill shrugged resignedly. "Well, we'll have to pick up that Black Devil's trail some time when it's fresh enough for my hounds to follow it. Nothin' else to do."

"I reckon you're right," Tom admitted. "But I want to talk to the fellow the boar ripped up. He—" He was going to tell about last night's attack, but decided not to, with Joab Lane there. "Who—who is he?" he added lamely.

"Never saw him before," Bill replied absently. "I sure can't figure . . ."

Tom hid a smile as he picked up Smoky's leash and mounted the pinto. Bill Tolliver was looking at his hounds in obvious disgust. It was plain to be seen that he

was more concerned about their failure than he was
interested in the identity of the black-haired stranger.
But it had not seemed to be the hounds' fault, Tom
reflected as he headed for home. They had tried their
best to find a scent. What had wiped it out?

Pete was now thoroughly acquainted with the trail
across the burn and needed no guidance. Tom let the
reins hang slack as the surefooted little horse chose his
own way. Smoky, now running ahead, snuffled at everything that interested him. As they approached the clearing, the tawny hound stopped and raised his head. His
dangling ears hung back on his head as he tested wind
currents that eddied up the slope. The familiar growl
rumbled in his throat; he had caught body scent.

A hundred yards from the clearing, Tom led Pete into
the shelter of the forest and stalked slowly forward.
Smoky walked ahead of him, no longer growling but still
reading the wind currents. Tom slunk behind a tree and
looked around it to see Buck Brunt's horse in the corral.
He led Pete back to the trail, mounted, and rode into the
clearing.

Tom stopped at the corral to unsaddle the pinto and
rub him down. When he reached the cabin, the warden
was sitting on the porch, lazily smoking a pipe. Tom
stared in amazement at Buck's freshly blackened eye.

"What happened to you?" he blurted.

Buck Brunt shrugged. "Looked through the wrong
keyhole. I see you had visitors."

"Two of them. Playful little cusses, too."

"Seems that way. Stirred up a hornet's nest, as you
might say. Anybody get stung?"

"Not seriously," Tom grinned. "What do you know about Hank Jamieson?"

The warden's eyebrows went up. "Not too much, except that Hank's one of the few mountain men who don't put me in the same class as rattlesnakes. He seemed willing to cooperate when I came in here, and tipped me off that there was going to be a raid on the Haystack Mountain salt lick. Somehow this Black Elk found out that Hank had tipped me off. A few nights later Hank's cabin burned. That's all I know."

"Then Hank's story was straight."

"What story?"

Tom recounted the night's and morning's events, while the red-haired warden listened gravely. He shook his head regretfully.

"Wish I'd been here, but the train was early at Martinton, and I missed Johnny Magruder. Riding back, I ran across a pack train. As luck would have it, the packer didn't see me, and I followed because I figured he was carrying contraband. I could have caught him redhanded, but this is the first chance I've had to see how the gang is getting their illegal game out of the mountains. Just before dark the packer hung up in a little wooded valley just outside of Water Tank. About ten o'clock he took the trail to the Water Tank crossing and waited there. When the 11:45 out of Martinton stopped for water, the baggage car was open. My packer started to unload his horses and I jumped him."

"What happened?"

"Three or four men I didn't see were also there," Buck Brunt said ruefully. "They had hard fists." He touched

78

his head and winced. "Also a chunk of lead pipe. When I woke up it was almost daylight and of course the train was gone. Still, I know how this gang of bandits is getting its plunder out of the mountains."

"Did you recognize any of them?"

"Cole Sellers, from Hilldale, was the packer, and he had six of Fred Larsen's horses. One of those at the water tank was Bob Magloon, a mountain man. I didn't get a good look at any of the others. The baggage agent, of course, is working hand in glove with them."

"Well, we know that much."

"Yes, and we can stop that much. If we can prevent them from getting their game to market, we can stop them all the way through. We're going to argue with those boys, and right soon, Tom."

"Think they'll load again at the water tank?"

"They'll load somewhere, and we'll be on hand when they do. They've thrown me off getting their game, but they can't cover up or fake their tracks getting it out."

Tom stared at him, then leaped up excitedly. "Hey! I've got it!"

Buck Brunt looked at him quizzically. "What have you got? Bats in the belfry?"

"No! That man the black boar hurt! Bill Tolliver's hounds wouldn't take the boar's trail!"

"Thought you said they couldn't?"

"I've got a hunch. Come on!"

Rifle in hand, Tom ran to the corral and feverishly began to saddle Pete. Buck Brunt followed, increasingly puzzled.

"I haven't time for wild-goose chases," he protested.

"This may not be a goose. Saddle up!"

The warden saddled his horse, and swung up the trail behind Tom. Sensing his rider's eagerness, Pete broke into a distance-dissolving lope. Smoky raced beside him.

"Hey!" Buck called. "I'm not riding a horse with wings! Slow down to a gallop!"

Tom reined in to a pace that the warden's horse could maintain, and held it steadily. He dismounted at the laurel and tied the leash on Smoky.

"Now what do we do, Sherlock?" the warden asked.

"If my hunch is right we do plenty. Come on."

Smoky walked beside Tom as he returned to the wallow. The hound's head was up, his heavy snuffling in loud contrast to the silence in the laurel thicket. The warden started to examine the tracks, but Tom put out a hand to stop him.

"Let Smoky do it," he said softly.

Smoky lowered his ponderous head to snuffle heavily at the maze of tracks. Slowly, with infinite patience, he went over the ground: out to the laurel, back to the middle of the wallow. He even cast a short way into the forest and returned to look questioningly at Tom.

"What's he looking for—a calling card?" Buck grunted. "If there had been a trail, Bill's hounds would have taken it."

"Wait!" Tom said tensely. "Come on, Smoky!"

Again, painfully slow, Smoky snuffled about the laurel. He paused in the center of the wallow, drinking deeply of the odors that only a bloodhound could find or recognize. His long ears dangled over his eyes as he walked to the opposite end of the wallow. He faltered, then went slowly on. This time he did not hesitate.

"There *is* a trail," Tom breathed. "Get the horses."

Buck led the horses behind the trailing hound at a slow walk. Sun had burned the mountain top, and scent lay so lightly that it was slow going. Then Smoky dipped over the side of the slope, where the sun had not yet struck, and began to strain at the leash. The men mounted, and Smoky broke into a lope. The scent he was following led back to and down the Klesa Trail.

The tawny hound reached the bottom of the mountain and followed along a creek choked with beaver dams. The trail was wider here, and Buck Brunt drew his horse up beside Pete. While Tom watched Smoky, Buck eyed the beaver dams anxiously.

"I hope we can bust this crew of pirates before beaver are prime," he observed.

"Why?" Tom asked absently.

"There must be two thousand beaver in these mountains, and they'll get every last one unless we can round 'em up."

"We will."

"I wish I could think so."

Smoky swerved from the trail into the brush, and through it into a small clearing. There he began to snuffle deeply around a small tree. The bark was chafed, and the ground around it heavily marked with hoof prints.

"Horses!" snorted the warden. "Don't tell me the boar turned himself into a horse and tied himself to a tree!"

Tom got down on his hands and knees to inspect the

tracks more carefully. He straightened up and looked at Buck triumphantly.

"This black boar," he said, "is really an unusual animal. You almost hit it right."

"What!"

"He's probably the only boar in the world who, after almost killing a man, would walk down a trail to this place, then get on a horse and ride away."

"I don't get you."

"The reason Bill Tolliver's hounds wouldn't take that boar's trail," Tom said, "is because there wasn't any boar. But there *was* a man—or rather two men—who had a boar's hoof and used it to cover their own trail. Smoky is a man hunter, and followed their trail when Bill's game hounds wouldn't."

"You mean the fellow you found wasn't attacked by the boar, but the boar's tracks were just to make it look that way?"

Tom nodded. "That's it."

The warden's excitement mounted. "Describe that hurt man again, Tom."

"Young, very tall, lean, and with hair the color of—of a charred stump: sort of dull, not glossy."

"Johnny Magruder!" the warden exploded. "That's why he didn't show up—he was bushwhacked! You took him to Bill Tolliver's?"

"Right."

"Come on! I want to be sure."

The warden mounted, wheeled his horse, and galloped back up the trail. Tom followed. He heard the baying of Bill's hound pack and rode up as the dogs swarmed around Buck Brunt's horse.

Bill Tolliver appeared at the door. When the old mountaineer saw the warden, his eyes grew frosty, his manner hostile.

"I told you not to come here," he grunted. "What d'you want?"

"You have an injured man inside. I have reason to believe I know him."

"You can come in and look," Bill said grudgingly. "That's all."

Tom followed Buck into the cabin, and looked down on the clammy features of the still-unconscious man. Without a word, the warden turned on his heel, his face distorted with fury.

"That's Johnny Magruder!" he burst out when they were again outside. "He did come last night!"

"Is this man a game warden?" Bill Tolliver asked in a strained voice.

"Yes," said Tom hotly, before Buck Brunt could speak, "and so am I, Bill Tolliver. And I'll tell you right now, I'm going to see it through!"

The old man looked at him, his face stony. "That man is bad hurt," he said slowly. As long as he's here he'll get the best care we can give him and safe passage when he can be moved. But you and me, Tawm Rainse, is on different sides of the fence from now on! Don't neither of you come back here. Now git!"

7

The Pack Train

In silence Tom and Buck rode away from Bill Tolliver's, up the mountain trail that led to the Rainse clearing. The redheaded warden was still too furious to talk, and Tom was occupied with his own thoughts. Bill Tolliver had been his good friend since Tom could remember, and his father's before that. Now that friendship was ended. A warden's job was certainly no rose-strewn path.

"If it takes me from now until hell freezes solid," the warden burst out, "I'm going to find out who got Johnny Magruder!"

"How do you think it happened, Buck?"

"Johnny did come to Martinton. He started over the Klesa Trail. He was bushwhacked there. It must have been by at least two men because one man couldn't do it alone. They used knives to make it look like the boar's work, and then planted those boar tracks!"

"To keep the law off?"

The warden nodded grimly. "But they didn't get away with it. Johnny's tough. He'll pull through, and maybe he can identify them."

"Say," Tom interrupted, "how'd they know he was coming?"

Buck shrugged. "Maybe they saw me sending the wire, and got hold of a copy somehow. Maybe Johnny talked too much when he got off the train. The important thing is, they didn't finish him. And they didn't get me last night, either, thanks to your dummy."

"*You!*" Tom exclaimed indignantly. "They thought they were shooting at *me!*"

Buck Brunt smiled wryly. "You poor nut, the Black Elk doesn't even know you're a warden. Don't forget I'd been using your cabin. That bullet was meant for me. So was the warning note that decided you to join up!"

"How was I supposed to know that?" Tom sputtered. "You didn't tell me!"

"You didn't ask me," the warden grinned. "I figured that if the Black Elk could persuade you when I couldn't, it was his tough luck. Want to back out?"

Tom shook his head sheepishly. "I'm certainly a jughead. But I'm in this up to my ears, and I'll stick."

"Good boy. Now, let's guess who shot at you."

"Whoever it was, Smoky tracked him right to that wallow. I naturally thought it was the man I found. But it must have been the ones who bushwhacked Magruder."

"I doubt it. Johnny must have started over the Klesa Trail long before that shot came through your window."

"But I'm sure Smoky tracked the same man *out* of the wallow that he tracked in, since that was the scent I originally started him on. Couldn't they have got Magruder *before* coming to my cabin?"

"That's a possibility, but we can't prove it now."

"What's next then?"

"We'll night ride, Tom. They're getting most of their deer and elk at night with a jacklight. We'll also catch those pack trains they're running and arrest anybody we find in charge. I want to get the baggage agent, too. If we can stop the shipments, maybe we can smoke out this Black Elk who's running things."

"How come they can get away with selling game?"

"The warden force isn't big enough or strong enough to stop them as yet, and the city police think it's our job. They're doing all they can to take care of crime in their cities without worrying too much about what happens here."

"Isn't that shortsighted?"

"Of course. The mountains can produce wild game and fish that'll give city people sport and relaxation. The mountain men can be guides and hotelkeepers for them, and make more money in a single season than they do now in ten years. Only there won't be any game left to hunt or fish to catch, unless wildlife is protected. That's our job, and it's a big one."

"Do you think there'll ever be enough wardens to stop violations?"

"No," Buck Brunt sighed. "The country's just too big. A thousand wardens couldn't put a stop to poaching in these mountains alone. Every one of 'em would have fifty thousand or more acres to patrol. The only hope is that the mountaineers themselves will finally wake up. Right now there's too much ignorance and indifference, as well as greed. Teaching them is our job, too."

"I'm with you."

"I figured that, but I noticed you had to get mad before you could see it my way. Well, we might just as well hang it up until late afternoon, then ride back into the mountains and see if we can catch a pack train. If we can, we'll pinch it and see what happens."

"Okay. That suits me."

They came to the clearing, let the horses drink, and staked them out in fresh grass so they could eat their fill before going out again. Smoky lay down in the sun that flooded the porch, and promptly went to sleep. Tom rigged a fly rod, while Buck carried a chair to the shaded side of the porch, sat down and propped his feet up on the railing.

"I've got another rod," Tom called to him, "if you want to fish."

"Not me," the redheaded warden declared firmly. "I never did like to hunt or fish."

Tom looked at him, astonished. "No nice crisp trout for dinner?"

"I didn't say I don't like to eat 'em," Buck grinned. "I

just don't get a kick out of shooting or fishing." He pushed his hat down over his eyes, then raised it again. "Be careful you don't take more than the limit. I understand there are a couple of very, very tough wardens in these parts."

Smoky ambled lazily with him when Tom went down to the creek, and dozed in the soft grass while Tom cast. A trout came up, struck half-heartedly at the fly, and returned to the bottom. Tom cast again and again, floating the fly over the place where the fish had appeared. No luck. The sun was pouring its heat over the clearing and the creek, and trout were not striking readily. Tom concentrated on the task he had set himself, working upstream and fishing very carefully. The best sport was when all an angler's skill had to be called into play, and this was such a time. An hour and a half had elapsed before Tom had caught enough trout for two.

Buck was asleep in his chair when he returned to the cabin. Tom fried the trout, heated beans he had cooked the day before, and shook the warden awake.

"Hey! Soup's on!"

"Oh, it's you," Buck grumbled, coming reluctantly awake. "It's too early to eat. I just fell asleep."

Despite his protest, the warden ate four of the six trout Tom had caught and heaped his plate three times with beans. He leaned comfortably back in his chair.

"I'll toss you to see who does the dishes."

"You lazy bat! I caught and cooked the dinner!"

"I can see you haven't got any sporting blood."

"I'll see you outside," Tom said heartlessly, "*after* the dishes are done."

Tom walked out on the porch and settled himself in the chair Buck had vacated. It seemed no time before the warden was prodding him.

"What say, Tom? Shall we ride?"

"Good enough."

They saddled their horses and rode off. Smoky walked sedately beside Pete as they pushed up the trail that led across the burn. Once through it, Buck put his horse to a slow trot, and cut off on a grass-grown branch path that took them through dense forest. They came out on the rim of a cliff that overlooked a broad valley. The warden pointed out a trail that wound through the bottom of the valley.

"They have to follow that if they want to get to Water Tank," he said. "We can see 'em if they come by daylight, and maybe Smoky will let us know if they come by night."

"He will. He'll catch scent farther than that."

"Then he ought to have a warden's pay, though I doubt if he could live on it. Let's get comfortable; all we can do now is wait."

They waited through the long afternoon and into the night. Far off, a wolf howled his lonely serenade to the night and coyotes started their evening yapping. The picketed horses stamped restlessly, and even Smoky finally wandered off to snuffle at some interesting trails.

Tom got up to pace restlessly back and forth. Wardens did not have an easy job, he decided, but probably the hardest part of it was this interminable waiting. Action of any kind would be far better than this. He sat down again, and glanced sideways at Buck, who was tense and grim. He guessed what the warden was thinking.

"How long have you known Johnny Magruder?" he asked.

"Since we were kids together."

"That's a long time. Neighbors, eh?"

"Close neighbors; Johnny and I were raised in the same orphanage."

Tom fell silent.

Then, in the distance, they heard the whistle of the night train out of Martinton. Buck Brunt sighed and got to his feet.

"They aren't loading anything tonight or, if they are, they've already got it down to the railroad. We might as well—Hark!"

In the distance a rifle shot cracked like a whip lash. It was followed by another, and another, until there were six.

"That's the Garson Knob Lick!" the warden snapped. "Come on!"

The Garson Knob Lick, famous for elk, was three miles away in a straight line but almost five by the winding mountain trails. It would still be quicker to take the trails, and ride, than it would be to attempt to go directly on foot.

They leaped to their horses and tore away through the night, disregarding branches that plucked like clawed fingers at their clothing or whipped across their faces. Tom could hear Smoky panting beside them.

The shots they had heard must have been fired by

jacklighters, the vilest forms of poachers. By day a deer or elk was a wary creature, alert and ready to flee from the mere scent of man. But by night they were trusting things that would stand and stare at a bright light while an armed man crept to within thirty feet of them. Many times a herd would continue to stand even after one of their number was killed. That nighttime trustfulness of elk would have accounted for the six shots.

At last Buck reined his horse to a halt, dismounted, and tied his mount. Tom slid off Pete.

"We'll walk in from here," the redheaded warden said softly. "They'll hear us coming if we ride. Will Smoky bark?"

"No. The most he'll do is growl a little."

"Good. Let's go."

Smoky walked a little ahead of the two men, stopped, and growled softly. Almost invisible in the darkness, he looked back over his shoulder.

"He's got their scent," Tom whispered.

"Be ready to shoot if you need to!"

"I'm all set."

A skilled woodsman, even if he was no hunter, Buck Brunt walked in absolute silence ahead of him. Soon Tom smelled the mineral lick, and saw Buck stoop to peer at it. The only light was a dim one that filtered from the stars, but that light revealed nothing around the lick. Tom reached down to feel Smoky; the big hound was relaxed.

"They've gone," Tom said. "They got away."

They walked up to the lick, a mineral spring that

bubbled out of the rock, and looked down at the pitiful relics that lay around it. The heads, feet, and entrails of five cow elk were scattered about.

"Too late," the warden groaned. "Will Smoky take their trail?"

"No. If they moved the elk out of here, they certainly had horses to carry them. Smoky won't trail anything except a man."

"I was afraid of it. Well, there's still one sure thing."

"What's that?"

"They didn't put anything on the train tonight. But they've got these five elk, and it's safe to assume they have more. Tomorrow night they'll have a load. We'd better be on hand when they try to load it."

They rode dejectedly back to the cabin, put the horses in the corral, and went to bed. For a long while Tom lay awake, listening for Smoky's warning growl. The tawny hound was motionless, slumbering peacefully. When Tom finally slept it was to dream of a nightmare in which five elk without heads or legs floated through the air. Just as he was about to get a shot at a man who intended to shoot him, the elk floated between and spoiled his aim. Then the elks' heads came out of nowhere to attach themselves to the bodies, and one spread its jaws to seize him. It began shaking him, and Tom awoke in a cold sweat, to find it was broad daylight.

"Come on, Sleeping Beauty," the warden growled. "Or do you intend to stay in your little bed all day?"

"What time is it?"

"Eleven o'clock."

"No!" Tom sat up guiltily and rubbed his eyes. "Why didn't you call me?"

"I did. Why, I've been up since half past ten."

"Early bird, huh?"

"Roll out," the warden ordered. "Flapjacks are on. You want more trout, you'll have to catch 'em."

Tom got up, dressed, washed, and sat down to the huge stack of pancakes and bacon that Buck had prepared. Smoky squatted on his haunches near the table, looking appealingly up at Tom and begging his share.

The warden toyed with a bit of flapjack, turning it over and over with his fork.

"Think he'll try to load at Water Tank tonight?" he asked.

"How should I know? You're the brains of this outfit."

"Sure, I admit that. But don't you ever have any ideas?"

"Once in a while. Right now I've got an idea that, if you wash the dishes, I can catch us some more trout."

"Go ahead," replied the warden. "It's a good idea."

Tom fished, and returned to the cabin with the trout he had caught. He cooked them, and they ate again. But the joviality of the morning had been replaced by tension. Tonight was the night. Tonight the Black Elk would surely try to put another load on the late train out of Martinton.

"Now I know what it feels like when a man's waiting to be hanged!" Tom blurted.

"Snap out of it," Buck Brunt advised. "You'll need a cool head tonight."

"Don't worry. I aim to have one."

"Just so you do. Have you got any buckshot loads for that double-barreled shotgun of yours?"

'Sure."

"How about letting me carry it? A couple of blasts out of that should cool off the most hotheaded poacher."

"Take it if you want it."

"Thanks. Let's get started. We'll head for the lookout over Water Tank again. The Black Elk shouldn't be fool enough to try loading there a second time, but I've got a hunch he thinks I won't dare try to stop him again. Tonight there'll be two of us."

They rode up the trail and cut off on the branch path that overlooked the broad valley. Before they reached their lookout, Smoky stopped. The big hound stood with one front paw raised, and growled warningly. Tom looked around at Buck Brunt.

"It looks as though we've struck oil."

"I hope it's a gusher," the red-haired warden murmured. "Take it easy."

Buck laid the shotgun across his saddle, edged his horse up beside Pete, and watched Smoky closely. The hound walked slowly along, his head raised to get whatever scent was blowing to him. They came to a branch path that led out of a shallow gully, and both men stopped their horses and dismounted without a word.

The trail ahead was scuffed and pounded, with little black mounds of fresh earth kicked up where horses had recently passed. Smoky strained forward, drinking in the scent, but at Tom's command trotted back to join him.

"Cover me, Tom," the warden said softly.

Tom stood in the trail, his rifle ready for instant use while Buck walked forward and knelt to study the tracks. He picked up and looked carefully at a bit of scuffed earth, then rose and came back, exultation in his voice.

"A packer with at least ten loaded horses," he announced. "He's headed for the trail to Water Tank."

"And—?"

"We'll let him get there. The rest of the crew will show up to help him unload, and we'll collect the whole works."

"What are we waiting for?"

There's no hurry. The train won't get to Water Tank until almost midnight, and we don't want to flush our birds before we're in range. Take it easy."

They rode slowly along, leaving the main trail and following little-known elk and deer runs that followed the general direction in which they wanted to travel. Far off in the mountains another shot sounded, but the two rode on. Now at last, they were hot on the trail of the big game they wanted. Anything else could come later.

They came to the head of a wooded valley. Buck Brunt dismounted and rein-tied his horse.

"There's a good view of the valley just ahead," he told Tom. "I'm going for a look-see. Wait here for me."

He slipped into the brush. Tom waited, keeping his eyes on Smoky. Presently the redheaded warden came back, his face puzzled.

"He's there all right. Same man, Cole Sellers. But he has only four pack horses. There were more than that. He's got rid of some."

"What'll we do?"

"Cole's certainly headed for Water Tank. We can get him, as well as anyone who tries to help him, when they transfer their load to the train. We might as well stick with the game that's already in our sights. We'll ride to Water Tank and arrange a little surprise party for Cole when he comes in."

"Sounds good."

They rode back to the trail, took a branch path, and soon came in sight of the water tank, a red tower on stilts, beside the railroad. Buck led the way into a bunch of thick aspens a hundred yards from the tank, and the two dismounted. They slipped the bridles on their horses, and tied them to trees. Buck Brunt looked between the trees at the tank, and then turned toward Tom.

"I don't want to jump Cole back here," he explained, "because I want to gather in as many of these jugheads as possible at one time. If Cole didn't show up the rest might not. But they'll be waiting for the pack train. As soon as they join Cole, I'll get 'em. You stay here and keep our horses from giving us away."

"How about letting me get in on the fun?"

"This is my business; I've got a score to settle with these birds. I don't aim to get in trouble a second time, but if I do I want you available for a surprise."

"Well—all right."

Twilight fell, and deepened into night shadows. At last Smoky, who had been lying prone, raised his head and strained forward. Tom leaped to the horses, ready to clap a hand over their nostrils should they show any signs of neighing. Buck Brunt slipped out of the aspens, toward the water tank. In a moment he had faded from sight.

Smoky's head turned with the approaching pack train, until the big hound finally looked straight at the water tank. Tom heard the sound of horses walking on a packed trail. A cold shiver traveled up and down his spine. Each second was an hour long. He braced himself for the expected sound of trouble. Then he heard Buck's voice.

"Come down here, Tom."

Tom snatched up his rifle and raced toward the water tank, Smoky beside him. Dimly in the darkness he saw the pack train, and against the water tank a man who had his hands raised. Buck Brunt was behind him, and Tom could almost feel the redheaded warden's satisfied grin.

"We've run our coon down and chased him plumb up a tree, Tom," Buck drawled. "Pretty, isn't he?"

"You've got nothin' on me," Cole Sellers said sullenly.

"There'll be something in you if you move," the warden assured him. "This shotgun I'm holding carries a double load of buckshot, and I wouldn't mind letting both of 'em go after what you skunks did to Johnny Magruder."

"I don't know nobody by that name."

"Of course not," Buck said sarcastically. "Just what are you packing on those horses of yours?"

"Firewood, and I have a right to."

"Sure. Sure you have. Tom, unpack the horses and have a look at his firewood."

Tom unlaced the diamond hitch that bound the pack on the nearest horse, took the tarpaulin off, and undid the basket rope. He let the pack fall heavily to the ground, and opened it. Astonishment filled his voice.

"He's right, Buck! He *is* packing firewood!"

"What!"

Tom slapped the packs on the other three horses, and felt the bulky wood that loaded them down. He turned to Buck.

"That's right. Four pack horses loaded with firewood!"

"Well, I'll be a jackass!"

Tom's voice rose in sudden excitement. "Buck, I've got it!"

"Got what?"

"Think of the other six horses! This bird was a decoy to throw us off! The rest cut down a side trail to Cat Bend; they can flag the train there!"

For a moment there was silence. Far off, the train whistled for the Martinton crossing. When he spoke, Buck Brunt's voice was suddenly weary.

"You're right, Tom. They've beaten us again."

"Not necessarily! There's a chance, a good chance, that Pete and I can beat the train to Cat Bend!"

"I'll go!"

"You can't! Your horse isn't fast enough, and Pete will never let you ride him! Here!"

Tom stooped, snatched up the discarded basket rope, and tied one end to Smoky's neck. He tossed the other end to the warden and ran toward the aspens.

"Keep Smoky with you!" he shouted over his shoulder.

"Be careful!"

Tom didn't answer. Sensing his master's impatience, Pete danced nervously as Tom slipped his bridle back on and leaped into the saddle. He bent over the tough little horse's neck.

"Come on, Pete. Run!"

The little horse stretched out, gathering speed as he ran and picking a sure way along the trail up which Tom turned him. The night train out of Martinton had to switch back before it came to Cat Bend. It was a slow climb, and almost six miles farther than Pete had to run. Tom spoke again to the black and white pinto.

"Give it all you've got, Pete!"

Almost without breaking stride the little horse raced up Cat Mountain and flew across the summit. In the distance, Tom heard the train begin to labor up the first switchback. Almost as though he, too, realized what the sound meant, Pete ran faster. As he galloped toward the long curve that was Cat Bend, Tom knew that he was in time. He halted Pete, flung himself off, and raced toward the railroad.

The faint starlight revealed a group of horses, and a man with a red lantern in his hand beside them. Tom slowed to a hunter's stalk. He heard the train gather speed as it came around the last switchback, and in the first rays of its headlight saw the man very clearly. It was Fred Larsen, the horse dealer from Hilldale.

Tom raised and cocked his rifle, and stepped out in the open.

"Who's that?" Larsen asked sharply.

"The game warden, Fred."

Fred Larsen took a nervous backward step, and Tom

shifted his rifle. He didn't want to shoot, but would if he had to.

"Drop your rifle, Rainse."

With a shock of surprise Tom felt the muzzle of a gun boring into the small of his own back, and cursed himself for a fool. He should have known that there would be more than one. Buck Brunt had told him to expect more, and in spite of it he had walked into a trap. Tom let his rifle fall.

"Lead Dather, eh?" he said bitterly.

"Right the first time, Rainse. You seem a lot better at guessin' games than anything else."

"Never mind the talk," Fred Larsen growled. "The train's too close and the engineer might get wise to somethin'. We'll handle him after we've put the load on."

"Move up," Lead Dather ordered.

The locomotive's headlight stabbed the darkness, coming nearer and nearer. Fred Larsen stood in the center of the tracks, waving his red lantern. There was a great hissing of steam as the engine passed them and throttled to a halt. As the men crowded up to the baggage door, Tom felt the hard muzzle of Lead Dather's rifle still in his back. He could do nothing.

The door of the baggage car was flung open and its light flooded over the little group. A man with a big tawny hound beside him and a double-barreled shotgun in his hands appeared suddenly in the doorway.

"It would be a good idea," Buck Brunt announced, "if nobody moved."

8

Brought
To Bay

There was a moment's silence, during which Tom almost forgot to breathe. Lead Dather's rifle pushed a little harder into the small of his back, and Tom braced himself. Then the pressure was eased by the menace in Buck Brunt's voice.

"I wouldn't pull that trigger if I were you."

Lead Dather tightened, then relaxed and muttered, "Aw, I was just foolin'."

"Yeah. All you boys want your little joke. Well, this one backfired."

"You got nothin' on us," Fred Larsen growled.

"One thing I've got on you is a double-barreled shotgun, and don't forget it. Take their guns, Tom."

Smoky leaped out of the car and landed beside Tom. The big hound stood tense and bristled. He could tear a

101

man's throat out with one snap of his jaws, and the two men seemed to sense that he was entirely willing to try it. They made no movement when Tom turned around and wrenched Lead Dather's rifle out of his hands. He took Fred Larsen's, and then retrieved his own. As soon as he did, Buck Brunt jumped from the open car.

Tom looked at him appreciatively. "Riding the train up here was a real inspiration, Buck. I clean forgot that it would stop at Water Tank before coming on here."

"Well, I didn't want to miss all the fun. Besides, I thought I might come in handy."

"You were sure right. What'd you do with Cole?"

"Tied him up back at Water Tank, and—We've got visitors, Tom."

Buck raised his shotgun, and there were two soft clicks as he cocked it. Then he lowered it again. Red lanterns shone beside the men who now approached, and revealed the blue-uniformed conductor, the overalled fireman, and the engineer of the stalled train coming back to investigate.

"What's the trouble?" the conductor asked anxiously.

Buck Brunt's tone changed to one of crisp authority.

"We're state officers: William Brunt and Thomas Rainse. We are confiscating an illegal load of game which these men tried to put on the train, and arresting the men. There will also be a warrant issued for your baggage agent, who is implicated."

The conductor assumed a belligerent air. "You mean Del Eastnome was in with crooks?"

"Exactly."

"I don't believe it, mister."

"I rode with him from Water Tank up here and *I* know!" Buck Brunt exploded. "He told me so. While we're on the subject, what do you know about these loads of wild game that have been going out on your train?"

"Nothin'. It's the agent's business what goes into his car."

"The agent will be permitted to make this run," the warden went on, "but from now on all trains out of Martinton will be checked regularly. If this man is found on any crew he will be arrested and the railroad will be charged with complicity. Tell your superiors that and get along."

As the conductor started to roll the door shut, the baggage agent staggered to the opening and stared out blankly. One hand was cradling his jaw. The conductor closed the door without a word, and the train crew boarded their stalled train and got slowly under way.

"You're very convincing, Buck," Tom shouted above the clank of the wheels.

"How so?"

"I suppose, on the way from Water Tank, you explained the principles of conservation to that baggage agent, and showed him how wrong he had been?"

"That's exactly the way it was."

"I figured as much. From the way he was holding his jaw I knew something had hit him hard. Shouldn't we have brought him along with us?"

"No." Buck shook his head. "I want something to hold over the train crews. I'm not sure just how much we could stick him for if we arrested him. The point is, neither do they. Let them wonder; the next time some crooked railroad employee may not be so quick to carry a poacher's load. If the railroad won't carry their game, these fellows will have to stop shooting it. There's no other way for them to get it to market."

"Good enough. Now what do we do?"

"Plenty." He turned to their prisoners, and Tom could sense the anger that gripped him.

"Which one of you waylaid and cut up Johnny Magruder?"

"Who's that?" Fred Larsen asked.

"Don't know him," Lead Dather muttered.

"Maybe you're telling the truth," the warden said grudgingly. "In the first place, neither of you have brains or imagination enough to get away with lying. In the second place, it would take more of a man than either of you, or both of you together, to get Johnny. Besides, if you had done it, you'd have used a rifle from some safe hiding place." He jerked a thumb at the pack horses. "All right, Tom, unpack a horse. Maybe these are carrying firewood, too."

Tom stepped up to the nearest horse and unlashed its pack. Smoky stood beside him, snuffling audibly at the pack as it fell to the ground. Tom opened it, pulled Smoky away, and stood up.

"This one's packing elk and deer meat."

"How about the rest?"

Tom punched the other packs; they were soft and yielded to his fist. Smoky sniffed hopefully as Tom investigated.

"They're all meat."

"They are, eh? Then we can proceed with the proceedings."

There was no mistaking the satisfaction in the warden's voice. For months he had worked hard, and at the risk of life itself, to capture the Black Elk's gang. Now he had at least part of it. He surveyed his prisoners with grim amusement.

"The rule book says very plainly that every violator must be extended all the courtesy due him. The question is, are the horses also violators? If we do not decide this just right, Tom, the whole case may be thrown out on a technicality."

A delighted grin spread over Tom's face. He considered very seriously.

"Yes, we have to consider the horses as violators, Buck. They're packing illegal game."

"You're right!" Buck agreed. "And the rules also say that every warden shall use the means of transportation which is most convenient. You have your pinto, and that pack horse you unloaded is most convenient for me. Of course we also need the load he was carrying, for evidence. All right, you two; get over there and shoulder it."

Lead Dather started. "You can't make—"

Buck Brunt touched one trigger of his shotgun, and a tongue of flame shot out. Buckshot pellets thudded into the cinders at Lead's feet.

"Both you heathens have shot enough illegal game with buckshot to know that it'll put considerable of a hole in anything. The next time this gun goes off I'll hold it about two feet higher."

The cowed pair walked to the discarded load without a word. While Buck continued to cover them with his shotgun, they expertly began fashioning the illegal meat into two big packs. Tom went for his horse.

When he came back, the two poachers had split the tarpaulin with which the load had been covered, wrapped the meat in it, and now strained under the weight of the two packs. Tom reined Pete to a halt and covered the pair with his rifle while Buck fashioned a hackamore for the pack horse. He mounted, and again leveled his shotgun at the prisoners.

"All right. You walk ahead, and don't be all night about it. We've got to be in Martinton by morning."

"This ain't right," Fred Larsen wailed. "I got a bad back."

"It'll be a lot worse by morning," the warden assured him. "Trot along."

The two started slowly down the trail. Buck, riding the old pack horse, lazed behind them. Tom followed on Pete, and the five loaded pack horses brought up the rear. Smoky trotted about, sometimes ahead and sometimes behind, but not going near the prisoners. After a half hour, Tom heard Fred Larsen's querulous voice raised in protest.

"I got to rest. I can't carry this no farther!"

Tom mentally counted off three minutes before the warden urged the prisoners on again. Then he did some figuring. The pack horse Buck Brunt rode had carried about two hundred pounds. Either Fred Larsen or Lead Dather was capable of packing a hundred pounds, or half the horse's load. Tom had often carried that much himself, but not over a steep trail at this fast pace. He urged Pete up beside Buck's horse.

"Don't you think you're being a little rough?" he whispered.

"Yes," the red-haired warden muttered, "but I aim to get rougher."

"Is it necessary?"

"You're darn' tootin'. I'm going to teach these birds so they'll never forget, that poaching doesn't pay."

"They seem to be learning."

"I hope so. It won't kill 'em."

Tom reined Pete in and let him drop behind. Maybe Buck was right. These men were not poaching just for themselves; they were slaughtering wildlife to sell. They deserved to be taught a lesson they wouldn't forget.

Buck Brunt let his prisoners rest twice more before they reached Water Tank. As they approached, Smoky scented Cole Sellers and growled a warning. Buck's horse, grazing with the pack horses that had carried the decoy loads of wood, raised his head and nickered a glad welcome. Fred Larsen and Lead Dather gratefully cast their packs down and eased their muscles. Cole Sellers called plaintively from the water tank to which he was tied. In the sad, wan light of a breaking dawn, the warden grinned happily at Tom.

"Go get him," he directed. "I'll watch these two."

Tom left Pete rein-tied, and went down to cut the

ropes that bound Cole Sellers to the water tank. The captured poacher stretched rope-numbed arms and glared at Tom.

"You and that redhead will hear about this!" he threatened. "Tying up a man just for packing wood!"

Resentfully he walked up to join the other two captives, who were sitting on their packs. The decoy herd that Cole Sellers had driven to Water Tank trotted happily up to join the new arrivals. Tom stood aside, keeping an eye on the captives, while Buck Brunt caught and mounted his pinto. He rode back up, balancing the shotgun carelessly across his saddle.

"All right," he ordered. "Pick up your packs and move."

"You ain't goin' to walk us in from here?" Lead Dather demanded.

"That's what I'm going to do."

"There's free horses." Lead Dather waved his hand at the decoy herd.

"Unfair discrimination," the warden said coolly. "Game wardens aren't supposed to discriminate between violators. Those horses were only packing firewood, and I just couldn't let you ride one. I can't discriminate against them."

"How about the horse you rode?" Lead snarled. "He could at least carry the pack."

"Can't do it. He told me on the way down here that he isn't guilty at all, but was forced to act as he did. He's an innocent party."

"All I hope," the poacher said fiercely, "is that you and me meet some time when you ain't got the gun!"

"And all I hope," Buck retorted, "is the same thing. Offhand I can't think of anything that'd make me happier than remodeling the shape of your jaw. Right now you carry your pack or I'll dust off the seat of your pants with buckshot. Move!"

Tom watched, but said nothing. More than once he had seen poisonous snakes helpless in the grip of a man who knew how to handle them. Now he saw another. If Lead Dather ever got the chance, he would strike like a rattler.

The sun rose, and slowly spread its heat over the caravan. The two men began to stagger under the weight of the packs they carried. Tom watched them closely. Even a horse might collapse if worked too hard with too heavy a load, and Fred Larsen was certainly weakening. Then, just as he seemed about to collapse, Buck Brunt stopped. Martinton showed ahead of them, crowded like most mountain towns into a narrow level space between two rising mountains.

"Get up there, Cole," the warden ordered. "Carry your horse-trading pal's pack for a while."

"I ain't—"

"I said get up there!"

Cole Sellers moved up to take Larsen's pack. "Are you takin' us in to town this way?" he whined.

"Sure. You know what they've been saying about game wardens around here: the state pays us for doing nothing. It hurts my feelings. I aim to show all of Martinton that some of you poachers can be caught. Quite a procession, too. Ought to make considerable of a stir."

They came into Martinton's outskirts, and Tom tightened his hand around his rifle. Riding into town with captive poachers might not be easy. The three men whom he and Buck had captured had done incalculable damage to wildlife in the mountains. Yet the bystanders who saw them brought in seemed openly hostile to the wardens.

The men and women who watched the little caravan had been reared according to an old American tradition. Their grandfathers, and even some of their fathers, had started out to conquer a wilderness with little except their rifles. They had shot what they wanted when they wanted it, and most of them had shot wastefully. In spite of the fact that uncounted billions of passenger pigeons and millions of buffalo were already gone, they still could not understand why they had to abandon their tradition.

Tom tightened his jaw and rode on. He looked to right and left, and saw only hostile or, at best, curious glances. Then his eye was caught by a shock-haired little man wearing horn-rimmed glasses. It was Chalmers Garsoney, the student of wildlife, and he was staring at the procession in astonishment. Tom grinned to himself. He was willing to bet that this was a form of wildlife the little man had never seen.

Tom reined Pete to a halt, and looked up at the brick courthouse in front of which they had halted.

"Come on in," the warden said amiably. "You can rest while we see the judge."

Tying Smoky to Pete's saddle, Tom followed Buck Brunt and their prisoners through the ornately carved doors of the courthouse, and down a corridor to the nearly empty courtroom. Everything looked dark and dusty, even the graying, black-robed man who occupied the judge's bench, and the wizened clerk beside him. The warden conferred briefly with a uniformed officer, who walked down the aisle and whispered to the clerk. The clerk rose and spoke softly to the judge. Then, with listless ceremony and what seemed to Tom an unnecessary number of hear-ye's, the clerk announced that court was in session. The uniformed officer strode back up the aisle and poked a stubby finger at Buck.

"C'mon," he said. "Hizzoner'll hear you now."

Buck led his prisoners down the aisle. Tom brought up the rear, watching curiously as the redheaded warden strode forward and stood before the bench.

"State game wardens William Brunt and Thomas Rainse," he said crisply, "with three suspects to charge with infraction of the state game laws."

"Let me see your credentials," the judge said.

Buck produced them, they were inspected, and handed back to him. The judge leaned back in his chair and eyed the warden placidly.

"What is your complaint?"

"Your Honor," Buck Brunt began, "for a considerable length of time a market-hunting ring, an organized crew that is killing wild game and selling it in city markets, has been in operation in the wilderness around Martinton. It has been my major duty to apprehend them. I refer you to the game statutes, Sec—"

"I know the law," the judge said. "Proceed."

"Last night," the warden continued, "Mr. Rainse and I discovered these men, and apprehended them as they were about to load butchered deer and elk meat upon the late train out of Martinton. We—"

"That's not true, Judge," Cole Sellers broke in. "There wasn't a thing except firewood on the horses I had."

The judge rapped sharply with his gavel. "Order here. What about it, Warden?"

"Seller," Buck Brunt admitted, "was apprehended at Water Tank with horses that were loaded only with firewood. The other two were overtaken at Cat Bend with six horses that definitely did carry unlawfully killed deer and elk. We have reason to think that Sellers was a decoy to throw us off the right track."

"What reason?" the judge demanded.

"There was a train of ten horses whose tracks were all together. Sellers left the train with four horses, for the obvious purpose of leading us from the rest."

"Present your proof."

"Well, there—"

"I was only packin' firewood to Water Tank," Cole Sellers said defiantly.

"Your Honor," Buck Brunt objected, "is it reasonable to suppose that any man would pack firewood out of the mountains at night, when he could cut all he needed near a source of transportation?"

"There is no statute," the judge said sharply, "that prohibits a man's transporting wood wherever and whenever he chooses. And your authority implies no justification for high-handed arrogance. You had no right whatever to arrest this man without proof of wrongdoing. The case against this man is dismissed."

"But—"

"The case is dismissed!"

The warden controlled himself, but Tom could see a red flush creeping up his neck. Grinning openly, Cole Sellers walked out of the building. The judge turned to Buck.

"I hope you have a better case against the other two suspects, Mr. Brunt."

"We have, Your Honor. Larsen and Dather were apprehended by Warden Rainse in direct charge of six pack horses loaded with contraband. I came upon the scene to find that Dather had wrested control from Warden Rainse, and at the time I arrived he was threatening Rainse with a rifle."

The judge looked at Tom. "Previous to that time, did you also threaten the defendant with a rifle?"

"Yes, sir. I thought—"

"Proceed," the judge ordered Buck.

"The men's obvious intention was to place their load upon the train for the purpose of transporting it to some city market and selling it."

"We wasn't goin' to sell it," Lead Dather broke in. "There's seven families down to Willow Bend as are hard up. We was just goin' to take it down to them."

"But you admit killing deer and elk out of season?"

"Yes," Lead said defiantly.

"The laws of this state were passed to be respected," the judge said sternly. "They apply to you, Mr. Dather, and to you, Mr. Larsen, as well as to everyone else. Nevertheless, I find some extenuating circumstances. In this section game laws are comparatively new, and it is common knowledge that many people are accustomed to

113

taking game as they wish. Such practices must be halted. I fine the defendants one dollar each, and extend the warning that if they are apprehended again on a similar charge, I shall not be inclined to leniency."

"What!" Buck Brunt exploded.

The judge rapped the bench with his gavel. "You are out of order, Mr. Brunt."

"Out of order! We catch these low-down skunks red-handed, and you fine 'em a dollar each and give 'em a warning! The game laws—"

"I preside over this court, Mr. Brunt, and unless you can curb your emotions I shall find you in contempt of it."

"You'd be right!" Buck Brunt roared. "I can find a lot of contempt for it! Why, you old—"

"Fifty dollars for contempt of court!" the judge thundered. "Officer, show this man out!"

"Buck, cool off!" Tom hissed. "This isn't doing any good."

The redheaded warden was wrong and Tom knew it, although he sympathized with him fully. He turned Buck around and began pushing him up the aisle. The warden suddenly wilted.

"Let's get out of this comic-opera court," he said thickly, "before I laugh."

Side by side they moved up the aisle. For the first time Tom noticed the little man who sat in a back seat.

"My," said Chalmers Garsoney admiringly, "you do have a terrible temper, Mr. Brunt."

⑨

Education

Buck Brunt and Tom strode angrily out of the courthouse, toward the milling, threatening crowd that had
gathered out front. Cole Sellers was haranguing the
hangers-on.

"The judge says 'case dismissed,' " he chuckled, "and
them two wardens couldn't do nothin' a-tall! You should
of seen their faces when he said that! I like to of died
laughin'! 'Case dismissed,' he says, and that's all there
was to it! Imagine arrestin' us for shootin' a couple of
deer! If I had them wardens here, I'd—"

Buck Brunt walked up behind him, laid the palm of his
right hand against the back of Cole Sellers' head, and
shoved hard. The poacher went spinning into the arms of
a fat man who stood near. He recovered himself and

115

looked around. Buck Brunt's face and neck were a deeper red than his hair.

"What *would* you do if you had the wardens?" he snarled. "Or what d'you think you'd do? You've got 'em, right here and now! Let's see what you'll do!"

Cole Sellers, frightened by the sudden unexpected onslaught, looked around for support.

"Maybe," the warden challenged him, "you'd like to come up and show everybody what should be done to a warden? Maybe you have two or three friends who'd like to help you? Maybe," he bellowed, "everybody would like to come!"

Tom touched Buck's arm. "Come on," he said quietly.

The warden shook him off. "You go on!" he roared. "Let me alone."

"Buck, this isn't getting us anywhere. You've got to cool off."

"Gar-rh! Not until I go back and tell that iron-skulled old fossil what I think of him and his tinhorn court! A dollar fine, and don't do it again or I'll fine you maybe two dollars! The prehistoric old crackpot!"

"This isn't the way!" Tom pleaded. "You're hurting us a lot more than you're helping. You aren't going to change the judge's mind by going back and tearing up the courtroom seats."

The warden reluctantly submitted to Tom's guiding hand. Awed by such consuming fury, the crowd parted to let them through. Smoky rose to greet them, wagging an amiable tail.

"What about this meat?" Tom asked, gesturing toward the waiting pack horses.

"Leave it for the judge's dinner," Buck growled, swinging up on his horse. "We've done our job."

Tom mounted Pete, and Smoky trotted beside him as they started out of Martinton. Behind them, they heard the boos and catcalls of the crowd. The warden paid no attention, maintaining a morose silence until they were well out of town.

"I reckon I made a fool of myself," he said finally.

"That you did," Tom agreed. "You aren't going to get anywhere calling judges old crackpots."

"Did I call him that?"

"You did," Tom grinned. "Also an old fossil. As our little friend back in the courthouse said, you have a terrible temper, Mr. Brunt."

"For two cents I'd send in my resignation!" Buck grumped.

"Then you'd be an even bigger fool. If you quit, the Black Elk is going to run everything his own way."

"We're the only ones who seem to care."

"We're the only ones who care now, but someday everybody will, if we can keep the game alive that long. You talked me into this job, Buck, but I'm beginning to like it. It's a big one."

"Yeah. With yapheads like Dather, Sellers, and Larsen running around ready to shoot anything that moves, including game wardens, and with judges to fine 'em a dollar each when they get caught, it sure is." He gritted his teeth. "I'd like to pick up one of those elk legs and go back to the courthouse," he snorted. "Then I'd like to belt that moss-backed judge with it. Every time I whacked him I'd say, 'Feel that, it used to be public property.'"

"Not today, though," Tom said hastily.

"Well, maybe not today.'

They started up a steep mountain road and the tired horses slowed to a walk. Smoky left the road to run down to a sparkling little creek that trickled beside it. He drank thirstily, hopped across the creek, snuffled upstream through brush on the other side, and recrossed on a beaver dam. Tom inspected the dam as he passed it, marveling again at the animal intelligence that directed such cunning engineering. Already, he noticed, the beaver were making their preparations for the fall and winter.

They left the road for a forest trail, and trotted briskly for an hour before reaching the branch trail that led toward home. Here in the forest the sun could not cut through, and Tom shivered slightly. To all appearances it was late summer, but there was a distinct chill in the air that foretold the autumn to come. They rode across the burn, down into the valley, and the horses broke into a canter as they neared the clearing.

When they stopped at the corral gate, Tom saw a note stuck on a nail. He read it aloud:

> I put the oats in your barn, Tom, and the grub and your mail in the cabin. Luck to you boys.
>
> Pop

Tom flushed gratefully, knowing that he and Buck had at least one ally. Pop Halvorsen, keeper of the general store in Hilldale, had himself been a market hunter in his youth. Now, apparently, he was no longer in favor of indiscriminate slaughter, and approved of game laws.

"Guess we've got one convert, anyway," the warden observed.

"And some oats for the horses," Tom added. "If you'll take care of them, I'll rustle a meal for us."

"Okay, but make plenty. I'm hungry enough to start chewing one of the logs out of the cabin."

Tom built a fire, and went out to the brook for a pail of fresh water. When he returned, Buck was stretched out comfortably on a bed, going through the mail Pop Halvorsen had left.

"A letter from headquarters," he remarked. "Maybe I've been promoted."

"Or fired for insulting the law," Tom retorted.

He poured water into the pot, dumped in a handful of coffee, took a back lid from the stove, and shoved the coffee pot over the flame that licked up. He got out the eggs, cut a dozen slices of bacon, and put them in his biggest skillet. As the bacon started to sizzle, Buck snorted disdainfully.

Tom turned toward him. "What's up?"

"Listen to this." The redheaded warden held up a letter. "It's what they call a departmental directive":

It has long been felt that a show of force by field wardens is both unnecessary and unwise. Violators who are forcefully restrained are often inclined to remain resentful and to commit further violations through spite alone. Much consideration has been given to the introduction of an educational program, which is to be inaugurated at once. Field wardens are to lose no opportunity to publicize their work, particularly by addressing church, school, and other public gatherings. It is also highly recommended that wardens reason with suspected violators, especially first offenders, and explain to them the principles of conservation, rather than to threaten them with arrest. All wardens are to act accordingly.

"Bah!" Buck snorted, flinging the directive to the floor. "Now I've seen everything!"

Tom considered. "I'm not so sure, Buck. It makes sense to me."

"Then," the warden grumbled, "I'd suggest that you explain the principles of conservation to Lead Dather & Company."

"That isn't what I mean," Tom said. "Lead and his kind never will change. Proper conservation still makes sense. Certainly there are some who will listen."

"Who?"

"That's for us to find out."

"Where are we going to find anybody who'll listen?"

"Oh, you're still mad because those three short-hairs we took in didn't get the book thrown at 'em. Can't we at least give it a try?"

"It's all right with me. I'd try balancing on one finger on top of a sixty-foot pine stub if that'd stop poachers.

120

Now how about choking off the gibble-gabble and hustling some grub?"

Tom lifted the crisply fried bacon out of the skillet and one by one broke a dozen eggs into it. He put plates and a loaf of bread on the table, and shoved the knife and fork box between them. Then he divided the bacon and eggs.

"Come and get it," he called.

Buck leaped up and looked hungrily at his plate. "I always did notice that, when a lot of eggs are put in a skillet, some fry up little and some big. How come I always get the little ones?"

"Aw, pipe down and eat."

They ate heartily, then Tom fed Smoky a mixture of food scraps and meal, stifling a yawn as he did so. A discordant buzzing filled the cabin, and Tom looked around to see Buck already fast asleep.

Tom sat down on the edge of his own bunk, removed his boots, and yawned again. There were things to be done. He should catch some more trout. The cabin should be cleaned. Instead, he lay down, and was asleep as soon as his head touched the pillow.

When he awoke, a faint light was filtering through the window. Tom sat up hastily, astonished to see that it was morning light. He must have slept through what remained of yesterday and all through the night.

He heard the crackle of a wood fire in the stove and smelled fresh coffee. Buck was already padding about on stockinged feet. The red-haired warden had completely recovered his usual good spirits.

"Hi!" he greeted. "Feel like going out and educating today?"

"Sure thing."

"Well, suppose the first thing you do is step down to the creek and see if there's any trout left that aren't too educated to get caught. I'm hungry."

"You're always hungry."

Tom took down his rod and walked through the dew-wet grass to the creek. He cast, and almost at once hooked a trout. He cast again, moved to another pool, and in less than ten minutes had six trout. Tom cleaned his catch, carried it back to the cabin, and gave the fish to Buck Brunt.

"Here you are, chef. Or do you think I should cook them, too?"

"Not this morning. I'm busting with ambition."

"Put some of it to work, then."

Buck rolled the trout in fresh corn meal, and fried them crisply. By the time they had finished eating, it was full daylight. The warden looked wanly at the dishes.

"Can't we just let Smoky lick 'em off?" he asked hopefully.

"Huh! Where's all that ambition!"

Buck moaned and started washing dishes. Tom swept the cabin, catching the dust and dirt up on a stiff piece of cardboard and emptying it into the stove. He was making the beds as Buck stacked the last dish.

"Want to ride with me?" the warden asked.

"Sure. Where you riding?"

"Over to Bill Tolliver's."

"Seems to me that Bill doesn't exactly love us anymore."

"I don't give a hoot if he does or not. Johnny Magruder's there and I aim to see how he's getting on."

"I'll ride along."

"Good. And now that we're out to educate people, Bill's a likely prospect. He could sure use some education."

They rode over the mountain to Bill Tolliver's. As Smoky stalked haughtily through old Bill's hound pack as usual, Tom looked at the dogs in surprise, then counted them. There weren't as many hounds as there had been. They rode nearer the house and saw a tripod made of three poles. From it hung the carcass of the black boar, head downward. Buck Brunt whistled.

"Wow! That's a lot of meat! Is that *the* boar?"

"It sure is! Wonder how old Bill finally got him?"

Tom looked around, to see little Sue Tolliver approaching, with both chubby hands wrapped in the loose skin of Smoky's neck. The tawny hound walked very slowly, careful not to upset her. Tom smiled down at her.

"Hello, honey," he said. "Where's Grandpa Bill?"

Buck Brunt slid off his horse, caught up the little girl, and swung her high in the air. Sue crowed with delight, while Smoky looked on, tail wagging gently.

"Somethin' you want here?" came Bill Tolliver's gruff voice.

Buck put Sue on the ground and faced the old man. "Hello, Bill," he said amiably.

"Well?"

Tom nodded. "Hi, Bill."

Tolliver said nothing.

"If the air around here will thaw long enough to let me put a word in," Buck said pleasantly, "I'd like to see Johnny Magruder."

"Five minutes," Bill grunted. "Doctor's orders. You can go in; Tawm can't."

The warden disappeared in the cabin. Tom remained on Pete, glancing uncomfortably about. He looked toward the black boar, and tried to speak casually.

"I see you got him, Bill."

"Yep."

"Lose some hounds doing it?"

"Yep."

Tom said impulsively, "Bill, why don't you stop it?"

"Stop what?"

"This moss-back, head-hiding attitude you've got! I swung in with the wardens because I think they're right! I know you shoot deer whenever you feel like it. If you kill a buck in season that's fair enough. But if you shoot one at the wrong time you aren't killing just that buck! You're also killing the fawns he could have sired! If you shoot a doe, you're—"

"Tawm Rainse!" Bill Tolliver bellowed. "Save that for them as needs it! I don't! I hunted and fished in these mountains when your pappy was in knee britches! I aim to keep on doin' it. I don't need anybody as wasn't dry behind the ears when I was a father tellin' me where and how to do it! You keep your advice to yourself, you little whippersnapper!"

"Why, you old side-hill gouger! I'll—"

"Are you two educating each other?" Buck's pleasantly sarcastic voice broke in.

Tom swung in his saddle to face the red-haired warden, who had come back out and was headed for his horse.

"If your business here is done, git!" Bill Tolliver spat. "And when that man's well enough to move, stay away!"

"Sure, sure, Bill," Buck said easily.

He turned his horse and trotted away from the Tolliver cabin. Tom followed, Smoky trailing behind. Once in the forest, Buck reined his horse to a walk, and turned to Tom.

"How far," he inquired slyly, "has our educational program progressed?"

"Not too far," Tom confessed. "How did you make out?"

"Your hound was right, Tom. It was not the black boar that got Johnny. He was coming over the Klesa Trail when something hit him. It could have been a club, something dropped from a tree, or a rock from a sling. He was dazed when the men closed in. All he knows for certain is that they *were* men."

"How is he?"

"Weak, but he'll come through."

"He couldn't recognize anybody, then?"

"Nobody at all. That leaves us a lot of open air to snatch at, doesn't it?"

"Looks that way. What's next?"

"Well, while we're here, let's go educate Trevor Gaylord."

They rode up a narrow side trail, and turned silently into a clearing. At the far end, beyond the cabin, a doe and two fawns moved like shadows. A man stood beside the cabin with a rifle in his hands. He was tall and thin, with pale blue eyes, a weak chin, and a lisp. He turned around with a start as the wardens rode up.

"We want to talk to you, Gaylord," Buck Brunt said politely. "It's about hunting."

"Yeth," Trevor Gaylord lisped nervously. "Oh yeth. I—"

"You know that it's out of season now?"

"Yeth. You told me."

"And you know that for every head of game that is killed out of season, there will be less next year?"

"Thertainly I know it."

"You wouldn't shoot out of season, would you?"

"Of courth not."

"And we wardens can count on your cooperation?"

"Thertainly."

"Thank you. Thanks a lot. This means a great deal to us."

"Oh, thath all right."

Tom and Buck rode out of the clearing and back to the main trail. Buck let his horse drop back beside Pete.

"I wonder," he said glumly, "just how long it will take him to find those deer we frightened away from the clearing?"

A shot cracked in the distance.

"Just about that long," Tom muttered. "Shall we go back?"

"No use. He'll have it hidden. I only hope he missed."

They rode every day or night, but the only fresh horse tracks in the trails now were those left by their own mounts. There were no pack trains going down to the railroad, and only occasional suspicious shots in the mountains. Apparently the Black Elk's crew, if not broken, was at least frightened.

Then one day in mid-autumn Buck rode back to the cabin an hour after Tom had arrived. The red-haired warden went to the wash basin, and began to soak his right hand in cold water.

"What the blazes happened to you?" Tom asked.

"Our educational program," the warden replied cheerfully, "has taken a great step forward. This afternoon I caught Trevor Gaylord red-handed with a doe he had just shot."

"So you tied into him?"

"Not at all. Not at all," said Buck, as he picked up a towel and gingerly dried his bruised knuckles. "I merely educated him."

10
A New Warden

In late September Tom rode Pete into Hilldale. Happily testing and sorting the various human scents in the road, Smoky ranged ahead. They broke out of the forest and into the little town's outskirts. Not since riding out on the day he had returned to the mountains had Tom been back to Hilldale. Pop Halvorsen had brought their supplies out, and feed for their horses.

Nothing had changed, but Tom was not surprised. A tendency to change was not one of Hilldale's most pronounced traits. There were the same houses, the same stores, and the same loafers sitting on the same benches in front of them. Shortly, when the weather became too cold to sit outside, the loafers would go inside and do their whittling around potbellied wood stoves.

Smoky trotted sorrowfully along, head down and the

tips of his long ears almost dragging in the road. He padded straight ahead, to all appearances a blundering, big-footed, awkward hound with no interest in anything except the scent he was casually following. Then Tom saw that, after all, there had been a slight change in Hilldale. At least the town had an outstanding dog.

From a side street emerged a bristled, stocky, yellow dog with short ears and a heavy jaw. It stalked stiff-leggedly toward Smoky, its intention to start a fight very evident.

Tom reined Pete to a slow walk and watched Smoky carefully. He had always known that every beast carries its own individual scent. A weasel, for instance, would run the rabbit it was trailing across the tracks of a thousand other rabbits without deviating from the one scent it wanted. Tom had never been able to decide to his own satisfaction just how one animal, getting the scent of another, could also deduce the other's intentions. But Tom realized that his own hound knew that the yellow dog wanted to fight, although Smoky had not even glanced up.

Tom watched the yellow dog come on, and guessed its history by its actions. Whether it had been brought to Hilldale by someone who considered it a good dog, or whether it had just strayed into town and decided to remain, it was clear that the yellow dog was a battler of renown. No doubt he had thoroughly chastised all the other town dogs, and now considered himself invincible. When only five feet separated them, the yellow dog rushed.

It was a bullying, overbearing charge that would have

borne the lighter Smoky helplessly to the earth had Smoky been there to receive it. However, though the tawny hound always appeared very deliberate, he could move with amazing speed when circumstances demanded. Now he sidestepped, and lunged when the big yellow dog was where Smoky should have been. There was an anguished howl. The yellow dog rolled over in the dust, then rose to its feet and, still howling, ran away on three legs.

The loafers on the benches, who had been hoping for a good fight, settled back disappointedly. Tom grinned. They didn't know that any dog able to hold his own in Bill Tolliver's pack had to be a fighter. Nor that any dog able to whip every member of Bill's pack was almost unbeatable.

The bench warmers made no attempt to hide their annoyance as Tom rode past to Pop Halvorsen's. He left Pete rein-tied outside, but took Smoky in with him. Every male resident of Hilldale who had passed his seventh birthday had a firearm of some description, and somebody might resent the fact that Smoky had put their champion to flight.

Pop Halvorsen came out of his tiny office to greet them.

"Howdy, Tom," he chortled. "It's good to see you. I thought you'd be back in the mountains huntin' a hole to sleep the winter through, just like an old bear!"

"Not quite, Pop. How goes it with you?"

"Good enough. How's the game warden business?"

"So-so. Buck and I haven't been making anything except routine patrols for a long while now."

130

"It has come through the grapevine," Pop Halvorsen said confidentially, "that you and Buck have stopped the Black Elk."

"Well, there hasn't been any game shipped out of the mountains for quite a spell, as far as we know."

"Good, good."

"It would be, if we had really stopped it."

"What d'you mean, Tom?"

"Something that's been worrying me," Tom confessed. "Neither Buck or I ever had our hands on the Black Elk himself. All we caught was three of his crew with a pack train of illegal game. We don't know any more about him than we did when we started."

"You scared him out."

Tom shook his head. "I wish I could believe that, but it doesn't make sense. Anybody who could run a market-hunting ring on the scale and in the style he was running this one isn't going to tuck his tail between his legs and yelp for home the first time somebody shakes a switch at him. I can't help wondering if he isn't just playing possum until he is ready to make a real play for some big stake."

"What's Buck think?"

"That we've licked him or scared him away. Buck's raring for a transfer; there isn't enough excitement around here to suit him."

"What *have* you and Buck been doin'?"

"Educating poachers. Every now and again we take— or rather I take—one into the judge at Martinton. I sort of try to keep Buck away from that court."

"You gettin' anywhere?"

"We ran up a real record last Tuesday. We caught Bradley Martin with a hundred and thirty trout in his possession after the season closed. The judge fined him five dollars."

"The fools, the dang fools." Pop Halvorsen looked through the window at the loafers on the street. "There ain't a one of 'em as wants to do anythin' 'cept set on his tail. If they'd go to work and conserve their game, instead of killin' it in the least possible time, in ten years this town could be somethin' 'cept half dead. Every train in would bring a load of hunters or fishermen, and put the town on the map."

"They still poaching out of Hilldale?" Tom asked.

"They allus will, I reckon," Pop Halvorsen grunted. "Mebbe you and Buck should do some educatin' around here."

"Maybe we will."

"The only way to do it," the old man said sourly, "is with a swift kick in the pants."

"That's Buck's specialty," Tom laughed, "and I must say it works some of the time. There are a lot of poachers back in the mountains who are very careful since they've been educated by Buck. Say, Pop, I came in to find out if I can borrow your saw and rig for a few days. Buck and I need some wood."

"Go ahead, Tom. You'll find the rig in my barn and the team in the pasture."

"Thanks. Will you fix me up a load of grub and some horse feed to take back?"

"Sure. Stop off when you've got the rig."

132

Tom remounted Pete and rode up to Pop Halvorsen's house, a little outside of town. Among other things, Pop owned a buzz saw and gasoline engine mounted on a wagon frame. It was an ingenious mechanical contrivance over which the old man had labored for weeks, and with it two men could cut more firewood in one day than half a dozen men with hand saws could work up in a week. Tom caught and harnessed Pop's work team, hitched them to the saw, tied Pete behind, and started back. He stopped at Pop Halvorsen's to pick up the supplies he had ordered and then drove on into the mountains.

He came to the top of a long hill and let Pop's work team rest. The tired horses settled gratefully back, lifting one big front hoof and catching their weight on the other three. Pete danced restlessly and blew through his nostrils, impatient to be off. Smoky stalked ahead of the team and stared fixedly into the forest.

Tom watched him for a moment. Smoky's head was high; he had body instead of trail scent. Tom wrapped the reins around the whip stock and jumped down from the wagon. Smoky looked questioningly around, and went forward when Tom waved his hand. Smoky entered the woods and headed straight for a trail that paralleled the road at this particular spot. The big hound began to cast, working back and forth but more interested in dangling branches that flanked the trail than in the trail itself. Tom looked at the trail. At least six horses had traveled it. Some of them were probably pack horses.

133

Reluctantly Tom returned to his waiting saw and engine. It would be wise to follow the tracks, to find out who was with the horses and why, but he had to take the saw to the clearing and Pop Halvorsen's horses were in his charge. Ordinary work beasts, they could not be left alone for any length of time. If they were tied in the forest they were apt to become nervous and if they weren't tied they probably would take the saw back to Hilldale.

As Tom started on again, some of his suspicions evaporated. Any of the mountain men might be packing in a winter's supplies. Or perhaps some mountaineer was stocking isolated trapping cabins. There were any number of logical and entirely legal reasons why a mountain trail should be marked by the tracks of six horses. Merely because horses had come this way, it did not follow that there was poaching in prospect.

Tom swung up the trail that led to his clearing. Smoky left him and bounded ahead. The big dog's tail wagged, and he looked as happy as a bloodhound could. He had formed a real attachment for Buck Brunt. The warden was forever slipping him tidbits from the table or rumpling his ears. Smoky still announced the arrival of other people with a warning growl, but whenever he caught Buck's scent he wagged his tail.

As Tom stopped his weary horses in front of the cabin, Buck sat on the top step with Smoky beside him. The warden waved a letter he had been reading.

"I went to Martinton to see if we had any mail there," he announced. "There wasn't anything except a letter from Johnny Magruder. He'll be out of the hospital in another couple of weeks."

"Good for Johnny," Tom said. "Is he coming back here?"

"He doesn't know. He may be sent somewhere else, now that things are so quiet." Buck stared listlessly into space. "You know, Tom, I think that whoever got Johnny isn't in the mountains any more."

"Where do you think they've gone?"

"Some place where they can have a free hand. I'd sure like to go hunt 'em up!"

"It won't be your fault if you don't," Tom said dryly. "How many requests for a transfer have you submitted this week?"

"Blast it all!" the red-haired warden exclaimed. "Those mullet-heads at headquarters haven't any business keeping me here! Anybody can handle this job now!"

"Maybe they've got other hotheads who like to chase market hunters," Tom chuckled. "It looks as though you're doomed to spend a helpless old age educating mountaineers, Buck."

"Says you! If they don't give me a transfer I'll resign and join the Marines or something!"

"Cheer up," Tom jibed. "There are fresh horse tracks in the mountains again. Somebody took a pack train across Stewart Ridge today."

"Probably a bunch of kids going camping," the red-haired warden growled. "There isn't anything else around here any more."

Tom unharnessed Pop Halvorsen's team and took care of the horses. The next morning, at dawn, he used the team to start dragging in trees which he and Buck had felled and trimmed. For three days, while a north wind blew and light snow fluttered around them, he and Buck sawed firewood. The fourth day Tom returned Pop's rig. Then, for more than a month, they rode routine patrols.

It was drab, unexciting work: combing the mountains, examining salt licks and other places where big game congregated for signs of recent kills, following signs when they could and, when they had reason to, searching the cabins of mountaineers who might have illegal game. Tom made several trips into Martinton with first-offense violators, and saw all of them receive light fines. Buck Brunt, with nothing but scorn for the court at Martinton, continued his own means of educating the mountaineers.

Nevertheless, even though on the surface it seemed as though they were accomplishing nothing, their work was beginning to take effect. Two wardens alone could not, and did not expect to, stop all violations. But bit by bit they were cutting the poachers' activities down. No longer did the mountain men, when they wanted a deer or elk, ride brazenly out on a hunt, then openly use a pack horse to bring their game in. Though few of them were cooperating with the wardens, they were all learning to respect them. It would probably take years, Tom decided, before the mountain men learned proper conservation, but he and Buck Brunt had at least made a start.

One windy day, high on a peak that overlooked a succession of lesser ridges, Buck Brunt beat his hands together to warm them.

"Tom," he complained, "I know what a canary in a cage feels like."

Tom laughed. "Five thousand square miles of wild country to prowl in, and you feel like a caged canary?"

"It's just that nothing ever happens here," Buck said irritably. "We've educated just about everybody except Bill Tolliver."

"I'd have visited Bill if I'd had any reason to suspect that he was violating."

"Yes, and you might even have taken him into Martinton, where the judge would have called him a bad boy and told him not to do it again. Where's the fun in that? I haven't even been shot at in more'n three months. Guess I'll ride in to Martinton."

"Go ahead. Maybe that transfer you've been praying for will be there by now. I'll ride back."

The warden rode toward Martinton, while Tom swung Pete and trotted him slowly back on the trail they had been traveling. It was still early in the day. He might just as well go home by way of Joab Lane's and see what Joab had been doing.

The trail followed the course of a tumbling little mountain stream. Reaching the valley, the stream leveled out into a succession of placid pools and beaver dams, some of which were already partly frozen. Smoky, who had been running a little way ahead of Pete, stopped suddenly. He lifted his head to test the air.

Tom slid off his horse. Even though whoever the

tawny hound had scented might be a perfectly harmless person on legitimate business, it would be just as well to find out what he was doing, and to see him first. Tom led Pete into some concealing evergreens and rein-tied him there. Staying away from the trail, Tom followed Smoky.

Walking slowly, absorbed in the scent he had picked up, the big hound started straight toward the creek. When they came back to the trail, Tom halted beside it and reached down with one hand to stop Smoky, while he looked both ways. Then he leaped across the trail and into the brush on the other side. The man Smoky smelled was near the creek. Since the dog had his head up, and had not changed his course, whoever he was tracing down had not moved.

Tom worked his way through the thick evergreens that bordered the creek. He dropped to his hands and knees, crawling beside Smoky with his hand in the dog's ruff. Tom peered out of the evergreens, and his eyes widened as he looked at the creek.

Roilly water poured through a recently broken beaver dam. The round mud and stick house in which the beaver had sought a refuge was broken in at the top. Wet mud flats surrounded the smashed house, and the fresh boot tracks of a man were all around it. Tom held very still, and did not relax his grip on Smoky.

This was one of the oldest and most despicable of all poaching methods. Beaver are aquatic animals. When alarmed they seek their houses, and are safe there from anything except man. But it is simple for a man to tear

138

out a beaver dam, then to walk to an exposed house and block the entrance. After that it is necessary only to tear the top off the house and shoot or club the helplessly trapped animals.

The man who had despoiled this beaver dam was evidently still present. His scent was plain in Smoky's nose, for the big hound was staring fixedly at a point just across the creek. Whoever had taken these beaver lay hidden there. Reasonably certain that he himself had not been seen, Tom waited. The other had to show himself, and could be arrested when he did. Then the brush on the other side of the creek parted and old Bill Tolliver stepped into plain sight!

Tom settled back, completely at a loss. Bill Tolliver had always taken game and fish when he saw fit, but he had always taken it fairly. It was almost inconceivable that the gruff old mountaineer would stoop to this. Tom remained where he was, not even twitching a muscle. Bill looked closely at the broken dam and house, then faded back into the brush and was gone. After ten minutes Tom got up and walked back to where he had left Pete.

If circumstantial evidence was valid, old Bill Tolliver had certainly ripped a beaver dam and house apart and had killed the beaver within it. Tom simply could not believe it. But if not, what was Bill doing at the beaver dam? Why had he been there at all?

A sudden thought struck Tom like a cold chill. Was Bill Tolliver really the Black Elk, the master poacher of the gang? Alone among the mountain men, Bill was capable of organizing and directing a market-hunting ring if he wanted to. Tom shook his head miserably. He had not arrested Bill at the beaver dam solely because he knew, or thought he knew, the old man so well. Bill Tolliver was simply not capable of doing a thing like that. Or was he?

Tom cared for Pete, put him in the corral, and glumly set about building a fire and making a meal. Smoky ran to the closed door, pushed his nose against it, and began to wag his tail. Tom let him out. A minute later, at full gallop, Buck Brunt came into the clearing.

The red-haired warden flung himself from his lathered horse and ran to the door. His face was flushed with happiness, his eyes danced. Buck waved a letter.

"Yowee!" he yelled. "Listen to this! 'You are directed to report at once to the Stone Mountain District. There has been evidence of a market-hunting ring in operation there. You are to investigate any suspicious activities, and to take such steps as may be necessary. Another warden will report to the Hilldale District November 3rd'—that's today—'who will be Warden Rainse's superior.' Wow! Ain't dat some'pin'?"

"I'm glad of it, Buck," Tom said, listlessly.

"What's the matter with you? Jealous?"

"No, I *am* glad. You need action. It's just that—I found a ripped-out beaver dam today."

"Who did it?"

"I didn't see anybody do it," Tom said honestly.

"Oh, you'll catch him. Some bird who wanted to get himself a few early beaver pelts. I should think he'd at least wait until March, when beaver are prime."

Almost bursting with excitement, Buck Brunt grasped his horse's bridle and began to lead the animal around the yard. When the horse had cooled sufficiently, Buck rubbed him down and put him in the corral.

"Keep my horse until I send for him, will you?" he asked.

"Sure."

"Then I'll go right away," the redheaded warden said. "I can get there a lot quicker if I take the train from Martinton. Ha! Something to do!"

"Don't you want to eat first?"

"Can't wait!" Buck declared impatiently.

He strapped his revolver on and gathered his few possessions into a pack. Shouldering it, he thrust out his hand.

"So long, you old mud turtle. I hope you and whoever your new pal is get these boys educated."

"We'll try. Good luck."

"Same to you."

Whistling happily, Buck strode up the trail to Martinton. Tom watched him go, then set about the preparation of a lonely meal. He had no appetite and felt dull and discouraged. Giving Smoky most of his meal, he glumly cleaned up and went to bed as soon as it was dark.

The next morning he was rested, but still low in mind and uncertain what to do. Halfheartedly he cooked breakfast and was just finishing when Smoky growled. Tom went to the door and looked out.

Chalmers Garsoney was entering the clearing. He walked up to the cabin and greeted Tom cheerily.

Through the horn-rimmed glasses, his eyes shown with excitement.

"What can I do for you?" Tom asked in surprise.

"A good deal, I hope, Mr. Rainse," Chalmers Garsoney replied, half apologetically. "I am the new warden."

11

Wilderness War

Too astonished to move, Tom just stood and stared. The self-effacing little man with the horn-rimmed glasses and the high-pitched voice was a game warden! Chalmers Garsoney, the fumbling, would-be naturalist, had replaced Buck Brunt as the chief warden for the Hilldale District!

"You!" Tom gasped.

"Yes, Mr. Rainse. I understand your surprise, and I admit that I appear to lack the physical capacity to cope with a great deal of roughness. However, I shall do my best to be a good warden."

"Well—uh, come in," Tom stammered.

"Thank you, thank you kindly," the little man said gratefully.

He walked into the cabin. Tom followed in a daze. Smoky, who had long ago catalogued the scent of this man, sniffed at him briefly, then padded to his own corner and lay down. Chalmers Garsoney removed his coat, laid it carefully across the back of a chair, and unbuckled his big automatic. He put his gun belt on top of the coat, and rubbed his hands in front of the blazing stove.

"Inclement weather," he murmured. "Very inclement. It is a real pleasure to be welcomed to as snug a haven as this."

"That's all right."

"Your welcome is scarcely as warm as your stove, Mr. Rainse. Allow me to present my credentials."

Chalmers Garsoney took a wallet from his pocket, drew out a paper and extended it with a flourish. Tom read it numbly. Garsoney's credentials were in order; in some way he had talked himself into a district wardenship! With awakening respect Tom looked at the little man, the top of whose head scarcely reached Tom's shoulder.

"By the way," his visitor continued, "I chanced to meet Mr. Brunt last night."

"You did? Where?"

"In Martinton. He seemed very enthusiastic about his new assignment. He said to tell you—I believe the expression was to keep your chin up—and he would be sending for you. He is certain that the Black Elk has centered his activities on the district into which Mr. Brunt is now moving."

144

"Buck will catch him," Tom replied absently. He had a mental picture of Buck's sardonic grin when he discovered who was replacing him.

"I fear not, Mr. Rainse. I am very much afraid that Mr. Brunt's elation will be short-lived. The Black Elk, whom he pursued so assiduously and whom he still hopes to catch, has never left the Hilldale District."

"How do you know that?" Tom demanded, coming back to earth.

"May I remind you, Mr. Rainse, that I, too, have spent a great deal of time in this region, engaged in my studies of wildlife. Because of this, and also, perhaps, because the local people knew I had no lawful authority, I have observed some rather shocking violations of the game laws."

"Why didn't you tell us?"

"And antagonize the mountain people? Not I, Mr. Rainse. At the very best their tempers are—er—shall we say uncertain? At the time I had no official capacity and no reason for acting. I did not care to invite trouble and thought it best to—ah—let sleeping dogs lie."

"Did you recognize any of the poachers?"

"I did."

"Who were they?"

"Two of the worst offenders," Chalmers Garsoney said reluctantly, "were William Tolliver and Joab Lane."

"What!"

"You heard me correctly, Mr. Rainse. Four separate times I saw Tolliver or those employed by him slaughtering elk and deer. I am sure that his house was the rendezvous where pack trains that carried illegal game to the railroad were assembled. As a lover of wildlife, such slaughter sickened me. I hoped against hope that you and Mr. Brunt would apprehend these men. When you did not, I considered it my duty to take action. I applied for a wardenship in the hope that the doers of such evil could be brought to justice."

"Justice!" said Tom indignantly. "You saw what happened in the Martinton court the only time we had a real haul!"

"I did indeed." The little man nodded sympathetically. "I admired Mr. Brunt's zeal and courage, but not his display of temper. It is my belief that this problem can be better met by—er—brains rather than brawn, if you will forgive the implication."

Tom remained silent, stunned by the news he had just received. Old Bill Tolliver and Joab Lane, almost the only two men in the mountains whom neither he nor Buck had even suspected of association with the Black Elk. This was fantastic! But was it? He closed his eyes, and again saw Bill Tolliver standing at the broken beaver dam. He clenched his jaw.

Chalmers Garsoney smiled. "I can judge your reactions, Mr. Rainse. What are your intentions?"

Tom said thickly, "I'm going to ride over and see Bill Tolliver right now!"

"No," was the quiet answer. "That would be a mistake. I understand your desire to solve everything as quickly as possible, but this situation needs some planning. Do you not see that, if you accosted Bill Tolliver at once, you would only put him on his guard? I cannot believe that Tolliver, whom I am convinced is the Black Elk, has abandoned his efforts to make a fortune on illegal game. We must watch him, and apprehend him in some overt act. We have no evidence that will permit us to hold him at present; any court must necessarily pit our word against his. As soon as we find a valid reason for arresting and holding him and Lane, we shall do so. Then, instead of charging him before the judge at Martinton, we shall take him to the hospital where Mr. Magruder is confined. I am convinced that Mr. Magruder will be able to identify them as his assailants. Then both Tolliver and Lane may be charged with assault with intent to murder. That carries a long prison term in this state, Mr. Rainse, and it will mean the end of the Black Elk."

Tom shook his whirling head. Chalmers Garsoney looked like a candidate for an asylum, but he was no fool. What he had just said was based on common sense. To go bullheaded after Bill Tolliver would only precipitate a fight in which someone was sure to get hurt.

"What's your plan?" he asked dully.

"A simple one. We'll keep Tolliver and Lane under constant surveillance until we find reason to arrest either one. I think that whichever one we get will incriminate the other. Suppose I take Lane while you keep an eye on Tolliver?"

"That's all right with me. But you haven't any horse."

"I am at liberty to use Mr. Brunt's, at least for the time being. And I am willing to start at once, if you are."

147

"Let's go."

As the little man started buckling on his gun belt, Tom looked at the absurdly large revolver which he carried, and shook his head in amazement. If his new partner decided to interfere with any of the hill men, and if they felt like fighting, he would have to shoot straight and fast to save himself. Still, he seemed self-assured enough—too much so.

"Hadn't we better ride together?" Tom suggested.

"Are you nervous, young man?"

Tom flushed. "No. I was thinking about you."

"I feel well able to take care of myself. In any event, our present procedure should be merely observation. Is that clear?"

"Okay."

"Very well. I shall ride to Joab Lane's and find a good place from which I can observe while remaining unseen. Am I correct in assuming that you will do the same at Tolliver's?"

"That's it."

They rode up the trail together until it split. Tom took the long branch that led to Bill Tolliver's while Chalmers Garsoney took the shorter way to Joab Lane's. Made frisky by the cold morning air, Pete trotted briskly, Smoky at his heels. A few snowflakes whirled out of the overcast sky, and the usual cold wind blew steadily. Tom eased the reins and Pete broke into a mile-eating canter.

Tom stopped him so suddenly that the little black and white pinto jerked his head erect and resentfully chewed

148

the bit. A sound like distant thunder had rumbled across the mountain top, and was spending its echoes on far-off hills. It couldn't be thunder at this season of the year. What was it? Tom waited a moment more, then snapped into action.

Now he recognized the sound he had heard as that made by exploding dynamite. Nobody bent on legitimate business could possibly have a use for dynamite in such a place. But poachers could be dynamiting beaver dams!

Tom removed Pete's saddle and bridle, and hid them. He slapped the little horse on the rump, and Pete turned back down the trail up which they had come. He would go home, and stay in the clearing until Tom got there. In the maze of ponds and brush where Tom was headed, a horse would be useless. With Smoky beside him, Tom slipped over the side of the mountain.

Another blast of dynamite shattered the stillness, much more evident now that he stood on the side instead of the top of the mountain. Tom halted to listen, and as nearly as he could marked the spot from which the blast had come. He knew this particular place well.

There was a gently flowing stream that coursed down a narrow valley, the sides of which were covered with a thin growth of aspen. As such it was a paradise for beaver. Their dams choked the creek from the bubbling spring at its source almost to its mouth. They fed on the aspen, and built their dams of the trunks and branches from which the bark had been peeled.

These beaver had been disturbed only occasionally by

149

mountain men who considered it worth their while to take a few pelts. The price of beaver pelts governed the quantity which they took, and for almost five years that price had hovered at a point where it was scarcely worthwhile to catch and skin the busy little dam builders.

This year, due to a scarcity of beaver and an increased demand, the price had almost tripled. Anybody who wanted to poach beaver in the mountains could make a fortune. He needn't run nearly as much risk as he did by slaughtering deer and elk for market, for he needed no railroad to transport his illegal take. One string of pack horses could carry countless pelts to another means of transportation, or directly to the market. If the Black Elk had decided to plunder beaver dams, there was nothing to stop him except two wardens.

Or, rather, one warden, Tom thought as he plunged down the slope into a stand of evergreens. Chalmers Garsoney was as ill-fitted for this kind of work as a rabbit for stopping a dog fight. If this was the Black Elk striking again, the mild little man who was now district warden would not have the faintest idea of the knock-down, drag-out, no-quarter fight that the poachers would offer. If only Buck Brunt were here! But he was not, and somebody was certainly dynamiting beaver dams.

Smoky stopped beside Tom and tensed into the wind that keened up the mountain. The tawny hound lifted one forefoot, growled low in his throat, and fixed his gaze on the place from which Tom thought the second blast had come. Tom slowed to a walk and began to stalk forward under cover of the evergreens. The wind that surged up the slope was carrying the scent of the men below directly to Smoky's nose. Tom did not avert his eyes from the dog, who was heading straight toward the creek.

Where the evergreens ended and the aspens began, Tom stopped for a full two minutes. Three hundred feet from where he crouched, the creek's usually placid course was a roilly flood. The water was laden with sticks, poles, and bunches of grass that had made up the beaver dam Tom saw.

Now that dam had a gaping hole. No longer shielded by the water which had protected them, the tops of the two houses that Tom could see were ripped off. He knew that the beaver which had sought safety in those houses were dead, victims of the dynamiters. Their pelts would be added to those which pack horses would carry down some lonely trail to a waiting buyer.

The poachers who had taken them were gone; only boot tracks in the soft mud around the houses bore mute testimony to the fact that they had ever been there. Tom gritted his teeth.

The wind, cutting across the valley and up the slope they had descended, was now playing tricks with the scents. Smoky faltered, then recovered himself and went on. The hound was working up the creek, in the direction taken by the dynamiters when they left. Now he was no longer certain of himself, no longer positive of the scent he traced. The wind was too swift, and too much at cross currents. Tom looked wistfully at the creek. If he could put Smoky directly on their tracks, the big dog would have no trouble in tracking down the poachers. He dared not; the thin, straggling aspens along the creek offered almost no cover.

They came to a place where the aspens bit deeply into the pines. Ahead of Tom, for almost three hundred yards up the slope, the straggling aspens had rooted out their own place in the evergreen forest. Opposite the aspens, the creek poured itself in a white cascade over a thirty-foot falls, and the ground rose sharply. To the right, and twenty feet down the slope, was a head-high bluff that dropped abruptly to the valley floor. Tom stopped again, and considered what course he should follow.

The poachers could be only minutes ahead. To go clear around the aspens in the safe shelter of the evergreens would consume precious time that he could not afford to waste. Tom looked again at the sharp rise in the ground. The open aspen belt was scarcely seventy yards wide. If he could run safely across it, he would be back in the protecting pines. Once there, he could overtake whoever had dynamited the dam without being seen. He decided to chance it.

"Come on, Smoky," he said, and started running as fast as he could go.

Blowing steadily up the slope, the cold wind bent the little trees and set their branches to humming. Instinctively, Tom crouched as he ran. He had estimated the aspen belt as only seventy yards wide. But now that he was among the little trees, they seemed to extend for miles, and he himself to be a huge object on a perfectly open plain. He must be visible for miles, he thought.

Anyone who happened to be watching could not possibly avoid seeing him. And there was no place to hide.

He was almost across the belt of aspens and within the sheltering pines when he heard a rifle crack up the hill. It was a sharp sound, as startling as a whiplash over a drowsy team of horses. Tom heard Smoky grunt, and knew that he had been hit. He acted almost without thinking.

Not breaking stride, retaining a grip on his rifle, he turned and scooped the big dog up in his arms. For what seemed minutes, but was only a second or two, he staggered toward the ten-foot drop-off. Unhesitatingly, but careful to land first and catch Smoky with his own body to soften the fall, he leaped down. Tom sprawled on the frozen grass, then immediately picked himself up and dragged Smoky as near as he could get to the sheltering bluff.

A fierce snarl, a sound he had never heard the friendly hound utter before, ripped from Smoky. He got up, wobbled unsteadily, and tried to find a path up the ledge. His fangs were bared; his eyes gleamed redly. Smoky was a bloodhound only in his man-hunting nose and his usual gentle manner. He was also half Plott hound, and all the latent fighting blood of that dog of battle stirred now in Smoky. He wanted to climb back up the hill and go after the man who had shot him. Tom laid a steadying hand on his neck.

"Easy," he soothed. "Easy does it."

Tom drew Smoky to him, and with his handkerchief cleaned the big dog's bloody head. Smoky held perfectly still while Tom examined the bullet wound. He sighed

with relief. The rifleman, shooting downhill, had mis-
calculated. The bullet had only plowed a bloody furrow
along the side of Smoky's head. It would still be wise to
take him back to the cabin and dress the wound.

Staying very near the overhanging ledge, and never
letting go of the dog, Tom worked a cautious way down
the creek. As he went, he planned his campaign. The
trail of the poachers would remain on the ground. If
Smoky was hurt no more seriously than outward appearances indicated, he could follow it tomorrow.

The poachers had invited a shooting war.

12

The Trail

Two hundred and fifty yards downstream the creek made a bend, and it was there that Tom left his sheltering ledge to take Smoky back into the evergreen forest. The tawny hound still walked unsteadily, and at frequent intervals shook his head in an effort to dispel the shock that lingered. Even though the bullet had apparently only creased him, it had struck with terrific force, and Smoky remained partly dazed. When they came to an icy spring that bubbled out of the hillside, Smoky drank thirstily, and Tom bathed the hound's head with cold water.

That seemed to provide some relief. Smoky walked more steadily, and now did not stumble at all. Tom climbed a few hundred feet and then let the dog stop to rest. He looked down into the valley out of which they had come.

Save for the fact that they were not prime, and were therefore less valuable than they would be in March, whoever had struck the beaver dams could not have chosen a more propitious time. Buck Brunt was gone and could not be recalled. He would be far back in the wilderness, where poachers operated. A letter or even a messenger might not reach him for weeks.

Tom climbed on, thinking hard. The use of dynamite showed that this was not any ordinary, haphazard taking of a few pelts. Every sign pointed to the fact that it was an organized and determined effort to kill as many beaver as possible. If the poachers were not stopped they could virtually clean out the beaver population in less than a month.

Tom reached the top of the mountain and stopped again. This time Smoky did not lie down. Fresh blood had bubbled out of the tawny hound's wound and matted in his short hair, but he was definitely feeling better. Not too fast, staying away from trails, Tom struck a straight course to the clearing.

When they reached it, Smoky ambled forward to sniff noses with Pete, who was cropping at the frozen grass. The little black and white pinto trotted up to Tom and brushed him with his muzzle. A guiding hand on Pete's neck, Tom steered the little horse into the corral and gave him a measure of oats.

He was certain now that Smoky had not been badly hurt, and that in itself suggested a plan of action. He would let Pete eat all he could, fix a big meal for Smoky and himself, then go back to the dynamited beaver dam and pick up the trail of the poachers. He would stay on that trail until he found the men he wanted, no matter who they were.

Tom let Smoky into the cabin, started a fire, and put water over to boil. Then he went outside and cut two big steaks from the quarter of beef which Pop Halvorsen had freighted in. Now that the weather was constantly at freezing temperature, it was possible to keep meat in quantity.

When the water was hot, he thoroughly cleaned and examined Smoky's wound. As he had thought, it was not serious, and should heal rapidly, thanks to the dog's hardy mountain constitution. Then he fried and ate a steak himself, and gave the other to Smoky.

Methodically he gathered food into a pack: bacon, bread, flour, dried vegetables and fruit, coffee, and a small skillet and pot. From now on he and Smoky would eat spartan rations and, except for a small bag of oats which Tom would carry for emergencies, Pete would have to rustle his own food. Tom tucked two extra boxes of cartridges into his pockets, then stood for a moment indecisively.

He should have help, but the only available aid would be almost worse than useless in a venture such as this. Beyond any doubt Chalmers Garsoney would be willing to go along, but he would only be in the way. To track down the beaver poachers would be difficult enough at best. The little warden seemed courageous enough, but

Tom doubted if he knew anything about trail life. Probably it would be better if he knew nothing about it at all; he might try to follow. Tom wrote a note and left it on the table:

> Dear Chalmers: I have decided to keep a twenty-four-hour watch in the mountains. Don't look for me because I don't know exactly where I'll be. I may get back to the cabin in a day or two. Leave a note for me.
>
> Tom

He looked to be sure there was kindling in the wood box, shut the door, and with Smoky beside him went out to the corral. The big hound seemed almost completely recovered from shock. Tom reached down to stroke his head, and felt a sudden surge of confidence. He was pitting his own ability, Smoky's nose, and Pete's endurance and speed against the poachers. It would be good enough.

Tom suddenly remembered that he had left Pete's saddle hidden on the mountain. He would have to make shift without one. He fashioned a rope hackamore, gathered up another coil of rope with which to stake the little horse, laid the rope and his pack on Pete's back, and mounted.

For a second the little black and white pinto stood uncertainly. He had been ridden so long in the orthodox manner that his saddle and bridle had become almost a part of being ridden. He was not at all sure what this strange procedure meant. But the only master who had ever ridden him was on his back again. He started off hesitantly. After a moment, becoming accustomed to this new way of being ridden, Pete responded willingly to the pull of the hackamore.

Tom balanced the pack in front of him as he rode up the same trail he had taken this morning. Now, the cold autumn sun was dipping toward the horizon. Tom buttoned his heavy jacket and glanced at the long shadows. It was too late to start his tracking of the poachers tonight, but he would be on the grounds for a very early start tomorrow.

Tom pondered. He could no longer choose just any night camp, but must find one where Pete could browse. However, there were numerous little clearings scattered throughout the forest, and most of them contained enough grass. He would camp when he came to such a place.

He stopped to pick up Pete's saddle and bridle where he had hidden them. Once more properly equipped, the little horse stepped along more contentedly.

They soon came to a likely site—a natural clearing in which no trees grew but where frozen grass was abundant. A tiny, spring-fed stream meandered through the middle. Tom drove a picket peg into the ground, tied one end of his stake rope to it, and looped the other end around Pete's neck. The little horse shook himself, looked at Tom to make sure he was staying near, and fell to grazing.

159

Tom made his own bed under the overhanging side of a huge, moss-covered log at the edge of the clearing. He built a fire, adding wood until the flames leaped and sparks shot like myriad fireflies into the darkness. When the blaze died, Tom felt the side of the log he had selected. It was almost hot to the touch; it would hold its accumulated heat for a long while. Tom threw some touch-pine knots on the fire. They would smolder without blazing too high, and help the log retain its heat. Spreading the saddle blanket under the warm log, he pillowed his head on Pete's saddle, and soon dropped off to sleep. Smoky was already dozing by the fire.

The night was still black when Tom awakened. He lay silently, trying for a second to remember where he was and why. Then he stiffened. Someone had a hand on his shoulder, and in the blackness Tom thought he saw the flash of a knife. He drew his knees up, preparatory to springing upon his assailant. Then he laughed sheepishly.

Smoky's heavy snuffling sounded almost in his ear, and the hound's cold nose was touching his cheek. His glinting eye was what Tom had mistaken for a knife. Tired of his own cold bed, Smoky wanted a warmer one.

Tom rose, threw a few more knots on the almost-dead fire, and spread the blanket so Smoky could get under it. It was an old woodsman's trick he should have remembered: when the weather was too cold for comfortable sleeping, take a dog or two to bed with you. It might not conform to accepted etiquette, but it was a whole lot warmer than sleeping alone!

Smoky pushed himself close to Tom, sniffing contentedly as he sought a warmer position. Tom gave ground. Smoky pushed again, and Tom once more yielded. A third time the big dog shifted position, and Tom came sharply against the overhanging log. With a satisfied grunt Smoky rolled over toward the fire. When he did, he yanked the blanket from Tom and wrapped it about himself. Tom sat up, shivering.

"Hey!" he said. "What goes on?"

Smoky stood up, the blanket draping over him to the ground. He wagged his tail, and the blanket with it. Tom had to laugh in spite of himself.

"I don't mind sharing my bed with a dog, but he can't have all of it! We're going to even this out!"

Tom grabbed the edge of the blanket, tucked it beneath him, and lay down. Smoky pushed himself close, alternately poking his cold nose into Tom's neck and enthusiastically licking his ear. Determinedly Tom retained his position. Even a dog had to go to sleep some time, and eventually Smoky did. Tom dozed.

He was awakened in the cold, gray dawn by Smoky's again getting up and dragging the blanket away from him. Shivering, Tom stood up. The fire had died, and frost rimed every tree. Pete's warm breath made a little cloud in front of his nose as he whinnied a welcome. Smoky walked over to touch noses with the pinto, then came back, squatting on his haunches and looking on with interest as Tom built up the fire.

"When I get back," Tom informed the hound, "I'm going to pile so much wood on the stove that the lids hop

161

off. Then I'm going to put all the extra blankets on top of me. Any fool hound that comes sticking his cold nose into my neck is going to have his tail tied into a knot. Get it?"

Smoky wagged his tail to show that he did, and Tom cooked breakfast over the renewed fire. He boiled coffee, drinking it black and so hot that it almost scalded his throat. While he and Smoky ate, Tom considered his course of action.

It was unlikely that the dynamiters had spent the night on the creek. But their trail would still be there and that was the all-important thing. It had to have an end. Of course there was always the possibility that they had taken to horses and could not be followed. In that country he didn't think so, but he must run that risk.

Tom rode Pete over the slope and down toward the creek. As they came into the evergreens, the hill became steeper and more rugged. Pete slid on his haunches, holding himself back with his forefeet as he chose a precarious way through the trees and around the various boulders in his path. Where the evergreens ended and the aspens began, Tom got off and watched Smoky.

The tawny hound was tense. He, too, remembered this place as one where he had had an unpleasant experience. However, though the wind blew directly into his nose, apparently he did not have a fresh scent. No warning growl rumbled from his throat; he did not center his attention on any one point. He still snuffled prodigiously, but he was evidently sampling the stale scent which the poachers had left yesterday.

162

Tom led Pete openly into the aspens and again stopped. Nothing challenged them. Tom stood still, boldly inviting any trouble there might be. There was no sign of life. Tom led Pete up the creek, to the belt of aspens that bit into the evergreens. There Smoky stiffened.

He did not growl, or give voice to any warning, so Tom concluded that this was merely a place of which he had uneasy memories. Letting Smoky go ahead, Tom led Pete slowly up the slope. Today there was no wind, no conflicting cross currents, and Smoky went directly to a stump at the upper end of the clearing. He stopped there, shoving his nose into the grass behind the stump and turning it over, the better to find any scent that might linger.

Careful not to disturb him, Tom stopped and picked up an empty brass shell from a high-powered rifle. He turned it over; it was a 30-30. The brass was not tarnished, and a faint smell of powder still lingered. Tom slipped it into his pocket. Whoever had shot Smoky had used a 30-30. Not that that meant much, because two-thirds of the mountaineers used the same caliber rifle.

Smoky did not hurry. Very deliberately he analyzed every particle of scent around the stump. When he left, he quartered toward the creek, where the lookout posted by the poachers had evidently rejoined them. As they approached the creek, Tom looked down its course, toward the dynamited dam. Between it and where he was, there were six more beaver dams. Not as strongly built as the one which had been blown up, the rest had been ripped out with crowbars or pickaxes. The tops of the houses were broken; all the beaver had apparently been taken.

Smoky turned aside into a thick growth of hemlock, and Tom followed. Grimly he looked at the grisly evidence there.

The poachers had stopped in the hemlocks to pelt their catch. Raw and redly naked, their flat, scaled tails still attached, twenty-two beaver carcasses were heaped in the evergreens.

Smoky looked back to make sure of Tom's presence, and went on. As Tom mounted Pete and urged him into a trot, the dog increased his pace. Less than a quarter of a mile ahead, the creek had its beginning in a never-failing spring that bubbled from the mountain side. The three beaver dams between the spring and the last broken dam Tom had found were also either blasted or ripped out.

The trailing hound swerved into another thicket, and Tom found the pelted carcasses of nine more beaver. He counted them twice to make sure of his tally. The poachers now had thirty-one beaver pelts. Tom stopped and did some figuring.

Beaver were of various sizes. Kits, or babies, weighed from four to six pounds. Blanket beaver, the largest, might weigh sixty pounds. Tom knew from the tracks he had seen that three men were working in this crew. Those three must have made several trips each to carry twenty-two beaver to the first place where they had pelted them. Now, with the additional nine beaver they had taken from the last three dams, they had a heavy load in pelts alone. It was unlikely that they would pack that load very far on their backs. Before too long he should find signs of horses.

He followed Smoky to the head of the creek.

Long ago, a fire had surged through here. It must have been a fierce, uncontrolled blaze in a very dry season, for it had consumed even the trunks of the trees. Only charred stumps were left here and there. Grass had grown richly among them during the summer, but was now brittle and frost-withered. It was a barren, forbidding spot.

Smoky halted, lifting one foreleg while he turned his head to the four winds. Tom studied him. There were apparently no fresh scents; the dog still seemed to be following old trail. Then the poachers must have separated for some reason which Tom could not fathom, and had scattered among the stumps.

Smoky bent his head and nosed around in the frozen grass. Tom dismounted, and got down on his hands and knees to inspect the place.

Something had been dropped here, but he could not determine exactly what it was. The frozen grass was broken and bent. Whatever it was must have lain here for some time. It could not have been a man; the area of broken grass was too small. But Tom knew from the interest Smoky displayed in the place that it had been something carried by a man.

Satisfied, Smoky lifted his head and again tested the air. Slowly, but seemingly sure of himself, he swung off toward one of the blackened stumps.

Leading Pete, staying far enough behind so that they did not interfere with the dog, Tom came slowly behind him. Smoky stopped at one of the stumps, and thrust his nose deeply into the matted grass behind it. He sniffed around carefully, again turning grass over with his nose in an attempt to get a better scent. He looked questioningly at Tom, then raised his head to test the wind. He was seeking the body scent of the man who had been there. Tom rein-tied Pete and went up to the stump himself.

A stray sunbeam glinted brightly on some object lying in the trampled grass. Tom stooped to pick up another empty 30-30 shell. On hands and knees he dug through the grass until he had found five more. Then he went around to look at the other side of the stump.

Three bullets had ripped into it, judging by fresh gashes in the charred wood. A fourth, skimming the side, had carried away a long splinter. Tom looked in the direction from which the shots had come. Obviously there had been a fight here, but why? Could there be two poaching crews, both of which wanted the beaver? Had they met in this lonely meadow, and fought it out for the possession of thirty-one pelts? Or had the three men he was trailing quarreled among themselves? He thought of the place where something had lain. Had the poachers who came out of the valley dropped their illegal load down there when they sprinted for shelter? Tom looked around for Smoky.

The big hound had left the stump behind which he had been working and was going toward another. Head to the ground, missing nothing, he snuffled behind that. Tom went over and poked about in the dead grass. He found three more empty shells.

He looked again at the first stump, a short distance away, and tried to reconstruct what had happened. Apparently there had been a running fight. Whoever lay behind the first stump had stayed there until he was able to make a break to this one. He never could have done that unless somebody else was covering him, and so far Tom had found no evidence of the other two. Yet all three poachers must have been involved in the fight.

Smoky left the second stump. Head to the ground, he started toward the evergreens that were here a bare fifteen feet away. Tom followed, and came upon the tawny hound snuffling about a patch of trampled ground around a tree. Obviously a horse had been tied here. Ten feet away he found where another had been tethered long enough to become restless and paw the ground. Here Tom picked up a handful of 30-30 shells. A little way away, behind a big hemlock, he found nine empty shells that had been fired from a .32. He looked back into the clearing with dawning understanding. Evidently two of the poachers had been able to reach their tethered horses, and before riding away on them had stood long enough to cover the getaway of the third. Where had he gone?

"Smoky," Tom called softly.

The tawny hound was on the trail of the horses, engrossed in faint traces of man scent that lingered behind them. Slowly, making no move until he was positive of his direction, he was following the scent. He lost it, cast about, and finally returned to the last place where he had found the odor of man.

"Smoky, come here," Tom called again.

Reluctantly the big dog left the trail he was working and walked with his master out into the meadow. Tom stood back, letting the hound work out the new problem in his own way. Temporarily confused by being taken from a trail, Smoky cast about aimlessly, then recovered his self-assurance. He went up to another stump and snuffled around it. Searching in the grass, Tom picked up four empty .32 shells. The front of this stump had also been pockmarked with bullets. Tom looked around into the forest.

He was now reasonably sure that the three dynamiters had here defended themselves from some unknown enemy. At least two of them had gotten away on the horses. The third was still to be accounted for.

Under Tom's urging, the tawny hound started toward still another stump, ten feet away from where the second man had been shooting. Smoky bent his head to the frozen grass; his tail wagged eagerly. He looked back, then sat down to wait for Tom to join him.

Tom picked up three more 30-30 shells there, and reflectively balanced them in his hand. Two of the poachers had been shooting 30-30s, then, and the third was armed with a .32. One of the former had shot at Smoky.

For a moment Tom hesitated. There had been evidence of only two horses, and apparently those two had been staked here to pack out such beaver pelts as the poachers might take. Two men had ridden those horses away. Unless there was a third horse somewhere, the third man had walked. He could not help leaving his trail on the ground, plain for Smoky to follow. Tom made up his mind, sprinted back to Pete, and made a flying mount. He trotted up to Smoky, still waiting at the stump.

"Take it," he ordered.

Eagerly the big dog raced into the evergreens, and for a while coursed along the top of the mountain. Then he dipped into a valley. Two hours later he approached a clearing that contained an old cabin. Tom dismounted, left the pinto rein-tied among the trees, and went forward on foot. Keeping out of sight of the cabin's window, he crouched along the wall and reached cautiously forth to tap the door with his gun stock.

A second later the door opened, and Hank Jamieson appeared.

13

A Prisoner

Tom did not leave the sheltering wall; there might be somebody else inside the cabin. And he kept his rifle leveled at Hank Jamieson. If there was to be any more shooting, Tom intended to take part in it himself.

"Howdy, Tom," Hank said nervously. "I—I'm glad to see you."

"I'll bet! Still looking for the men who burned your cabin?"

"That's it, Tom. I trailed 'em here and—"

"Never mind!" Tom snapped. "It won't work a second time!"

"Uh—what won't?"

"The wonderful little story I was too dumb to see through the first time you told me! Who's inside?"

"Nobody."

"Turn around, Hank."

The mountaineer paled. "You wouldn't," he quavered, "shoot a man in the back?"

"Turn around and walk into the cabin. If there's anybody else in there, and they try anything, you get it first—right between the shoulder blades."

"There—there ain't nobody else here."

"We'll find out."

Hank Jamieson turned around and walked into the cabin. Tom followed, with Smoky trailing behind him. A sweeping glance around the cabin's one room revealed nobody else.

The mountaineer's forehead was beaded with sweat. "What you goin' to do?" he asked nervously.

"The very least I'm going to do is charge you with dynamiting beaver dams. You're under arrest. What else I'm going to do depends on a lot of things."

"I didn't dynamite no dams."

"You're lying, Hank." Tom looked at the rifle standing in one corner of the cabin. "Is that the 30-30 you shot at Smoky with yesterday?"

"That wasn't me!"

"Who was it?"

"I dunno. Tom, if you lemme go I swear I'll never do anythin' again! I swear it!"

"Hank, I wouldn't take your word for the time of day. And you can't lie or wriggle your way out of this one. I know exactly what you've been doing since yesterday. You and two others were dynamiting beaver dams in

171

Sugar Bowl Creek. You got thirty-one beaver. In the meadow at the head of the creek, somebody jumped you and you had to shoot it out. Right?"

"I wasn't anywheres near—"

"Right?" Tom snarled.

"That—that's right."

"Who was with you?"

"Tom, if they ever find out I told you, they'll kill me!"

"And if you don't tell, I will! Who was with you in that meadow?"

"Lead Dather and Bob Magloon."

"Who shot at Smoky?"

"It wasn't me!" Hank Jamieson said desperately. "I swear it wasn't! It was Lead!"

"You'd better be telling the truth," Tom gritted.

"I am!"

"Now tell me something else. When you knew perfectly well I was around these parts, why were you dumb enough to dynamite beaver dams in broad daylight? Didn't you figure I had ears?"

Hank Jamieson said sullenly, "The Black Elk said he had took care of the wardens."

"Then you *are* working for the Black Elk? Who is he?"

"I don't know!"

"You're lying!"

"I'm not and I swear I'm not! I never even seen him."

"Who gave you your orders?"

"Lead Dather," Hank Jamieson moaned. "Oh, why did I ever get into this mess?"

"It's a poor time to ask that," Tom said grimly. "Tell me the story, and it had better be straight."

"I'll tell you," Hank said miserably. "I might as well. 'Twas Lead Dather who come to me and asked how I'd like to earn a lot of money. I told him sure, money's hard to come by. Then he told me how I could do it."

"How?"

"By shootin' and skinnin' deer and elk and packin' 'em down to the railroad."

"Didn't you know that was illegal?"

"Sure, but there was good money in it. Some weeks I earnt as much as a hun'ert dollars, and I had to go out only two or three nights a week. Well, when Lead come to me I asked him if we wasn't likely to get caught. He said he didn't think so, but he had a right smart notion. We would burn my cabin, he said, and spread the story that I had been burnt out by the Black Elk. Then nobody would ever think I was workin' for him. It sounded good, see, and all I had to do was hunt and pack. I like to hunt."

"Go on."

"Things run real good for quite a spell, then that redheaded warden started messin' 'em up. Lead says the Black Elk wanted to get rid of him, so we give him forty-eight hours to leave. If he didn't leave, we was to shoot at him. Lead says I was the most likely one to do it, and if I got caught I should say I'd been huntin' the Black Elk. That tied in, see? Everybody knowed I was mad at him for burnin' my cabin."

"What did Lead promise you for it?"

"He said my cut would be raised; I'd get more money."

Tom shivered. This gang was even more ruthless than he had thought.

"Then it was you who fired the first shot through my cabin window that night?"

"Yes, but I knew it was a dummy. Honest I did! I just wanted to scare the redhead!"

"Who fired the second shot?"

"I don't know."

"You don't know!"

"I'm tellin' you the truth, so help me! I still don't know who 'twas!"

"Why didn't they try again after they found out they'd failed?"

"On account of that dog of yours. Every time anybody tried to come near he'd give 'em away."

"But you kept right on market hunting anyway?"

"Sure. Lead says you couldn't stop us with a dog. Then, after you got Lead, Cole and Fred Larsen, the Black Elk give orders to lay low."

"I thought you don't know the Black Elk?"

"I don't. I never seen him, I tell you. The orders come through Lead. He says we'd hit the beaver hard when fall come and make up for all the money we was losin'."

"Weren't you worried about us when you went after beaver?"

"Lead says there wasn't nothin' to worry about. He says the red-head was gettin' sent some place else and that you couldn't do nothin' by yourself."

"Lead said that? How'd he know Brunt was being transferred?"

"I dunno. But he says that everythin' was sewed up,

174

and that even if you did raise a ruckus, it was all took care of. He says we was safe as we would be in church."

Tom was silent for a moment, digesting the news he had received. How was it possible for this poaching gang to know that Buck Brunt had been transferred? Did they know about Garsoney? If so, the little man was in more danger than he knew. This gang would stop at nothing.

"Who jumped you when you came out of Sugar Bowl?" he asked suddenly.

"Bill Tolliver."

"Are you sure?"

Hank Jamieson nodded emphatically. "There ain't no mistakin' it; I saw him. He whanged away at us as soon as we broke cover, and his first shot parted Bob's hair. We dropped our pelts and sprinted for cover. We was able to keep him pinned down until we got away."

"You're lying again!" Tom said hotly. "This time I know you are."

"I'm not!"

"Yes you are! If Bill Tolliver had had a fair shot at any of you, he would have killed you."

"'Twas gettin' dark when we come out of Sugar Bowl," Hank explained. He shuddered. "It wa'nt a good shootin' light, or mebbe he would of got all of us."

Tom said fiercely, "Tell me one thing, and I'll throttle you if you lie! Is Bill Tolliver the Black Elk?"

"I told you I never seen the Black Elk."

"Did you ever have reason to think it was Bill?"

"Could be. How should I know?"

"Come on, Hank," Tom said grimly.

"Where we goin'?"

175

"Over to see Bill Tolliver."

"Not me! He'll kill me!"

"Somebody should have done that long ago. Come on."

"I—I ain't got no horse."

"Nobody said anything about you riding. You're going to walk. You're going to face Bill Tolliver with everything you told me."

"It's all true! Can't you take my word for it, Tom?"

"No! Are you coming, or am I going to hoist you along by the seat of your britches?"

Hesitantly, Hank walked out of the cabin. Keeping a wary eye on his prisoner, Tom mounted Pete. Smoky waited until Tom was ready, then padded along beside the pinto. Hank looked back pleadingly. Tom waved his rifle, and the mountain man started reluctantly down the trail.

Keeping Pete at a walk, Tom followed, thinking furiously. He had one member of the Black Elk's gang. Who were the rest, besides Lead Dather, Bob Magloon, Cole Sellers, and Fred Larsen? Above all, who was the Black Elk? Was Bill Tolliver really the leader of the gang, and if so why had he chosen to pick a fight with three of his own men? Had they betrayed him in some way, or had he thought that they were about to? Were there two poaching gangs at war with each other, and was Bill Tolliver the Black Elk's rival? Tom was positive only of one thing. He had picked this trail up at the dynamited beaver dam, and would find the end of it.

They rode down the valley toward Bill's house. As they approached the clearing, Smoky stopped suddenly, sniffed the air, and growled. Tom stopped. Smoky wouldn't growl at any of the Tollivers; there must be a stranger with them.

Hearing the dog growl, Hank Jamieson also stopped and looked around questioningly.

"There may be trouble, Hank," Tom warned. "If it's one of your friends, and you try to make a break, you'll be the first to get it. Now get going."

They entered the clearing, and made their way through Bill's bellowing hound pack. The old man appeared at the door.

"What's goin' on here, Tawm?" he demanded.

As Tom started to reply, he caught sight of a tall, dark-haired man behind Bill Tolliver. The stranger pushed his way past Bill, and Tom swung his rifle around to cover the door.

"You must be Tom Rainse," the black-haired man said, limping out on the porch. "Don't you recognize me? I'm Johnny Magruder."

Tom stared at him, speechless. If he had said he was the Black Elk, Tom would have been no more surprised. What was Johnny Magruder doing back at the Tollivers'?

Johnny grinned at him. "I was on my way to see you and Buck, but decided to stop in here first. How is the old redheaded fireball?"

"He's—he's been transferred," Tom stammered, still bewildered. "But what—"

"Somethin' you wanted of me, Tawm?" Bill Tolliver rumbled.

Tom snapped back to the world he lived in, and the

177

business at hand. Dismounting, he indicated Hank Jamieson.

"Yes, there is, Bill. I want to know why you fought three men at the head of Sugar Bowl Creek last night. Hank, here, claims he was one of them."

"It was dark and I couldn't swear to it," Bill Tolliver mumbled. "He might have been one. All I know is that there was three of 'em, and that they had a big bunch of beaver pelts."

Johnny Magruder swung fiercely on the old man. "Bill, you promised you'd wait!"

"Say," Tom exploded. "Just what's going on here?"

"Bill told me today about the beaver poaching," Johnny explained, "but he said he'd wait for you and Buck so it could be stopped legally."

"When there's varmints around," Bill Tolliver muttered, "you got to get 'em when you've got a chance. They'd already cleaned out the beaver in Harkway Crick, and here they was workin' on Sugar Bowl."

"Wait a minute," Tom interrupted. "As I remember it, you didn't like wardens!"

"Man's got a right to change his mind," Bill grunted sheepishly. "Besides, I had this Johnny Magruder in my house for two weeks, and he talked a lot of sense. You young'uns have got to have a chance in these mountains, same as I did. Won't be no game for anybody if this poachin' ain't stopped."

"Why, you old coot!" Tom cried, torn between exasperation and relief. "Why didn't you tell me?"

"I figured if you was too bullheaded to come talk things over, you could set where you was."

"But I did! I told you the same—"

"Bill!"

It was a desperate, heartrending cry from the other end of the clearing. They swung around, to see Elaine Tolliver running toward them as fast as her exhausted legs could carry her.

"Bill!" she gasped. "They've got Sue!"

14

The Black Elk

For what seemed a long time, no one said a word. The only sound was Elaine's labored breathing as she tried to catch her breath.

"Who's got her, honey?" Bill Tolliver said gently.

"I don't know," Elaine panted. "I didn't see them. Sue and I were getting pine branches. They came from behind. One held me while the other made off with Sue. I—I could hear her crying."

"Couldn't tell who it was, eh?"

Elaine shook her head. "The one holding me shoved me into the tree when he ran. When I turned around, he'd ducked into the pines and I just saw his back." Her voice trembled. "They said—they said if you left them alone she'd be all right."

"They did, did they?" Bill Tolliver said slowly. "They

picked the wrong man. I'm ridin', right now. Don't you fret, Elaine. Sue is comin' back safe."

"I'm going with you, Bill," Tom said. "This is my job, too."

"Think you can travel hard and fast, boy?"

"I'll keep up. The trail is fresh and Smoky will take it."

The old man shook his massive head. "No good, Tawm. They're sure to have horses."

Tom's face fell. It was true. They would have horses, of course. As soon as they mounted them, the man-scent would disappear and Smoky would be thrown off, baffled.

Johnny Magruder spoke up. "You've had that hound on a man's trail before, and he took it?"

"Plenty of them," Tom said. "He even tracked the men who got you until they took to horses."

"Didn't you give him a chance to work the trail out?"

"What do you mean?"

"If he's a bloodhound, and will follow a foot scent, he will also track the same scent even though its owner takes to a horse. The scent stays. Didn't you know that?"

Tom and Bill Tolliver looked at each other. They were hunters of game, and the scents their hounds usually followed were plainly imprinted upon the earth.

"Do you mean the scent clings to leaves and brush, or sort of hangs in the air?" Tom asked.

"That's the idea. Nobody knows for sure. But let the dog work it out in his own way."

Bill Tolliver shook his head incredulously. "Mebbe so; we'll try it, Tawm. But we're wastin' time. I'll saddle up."

"I'm going too!" Johnny Magruder declared.

"Not you, Johnny," Bill Tolliver called over his shoulder as he headed for the corral. "You'll just slow us down."

Tom indicated Hank Jamieson, still standing in dejected silence. "I've got one of 'em here, Johnny, and you can see that he stays here. He's charged with dynamiting beaver dams plus whatever else I can stick him with. How about watching him?"

"I will!" Johnny Magruder promised grimly.

Bill Tolliver led up his big white horse and disappeared into the cabin to reappear almost instantly, a rifle in his hand.

"Where'd they jump you, honey?" he asked Elaine.

"North of the spring, in that grove of young pines. We were just off the trail."

The old man nodded. "We'll get her. Don't fret now. Come on, Tawm."

"Good luck," Johnny called enviously.

They swung into their saddles and galloped out of the clearing, Smoky racing beside them.

In spite of Sue's capture, Tom felt a tremendous relief. Bill Tolliver was not only cleared of suspicion, but had been fighting the poachers on his own initiative. They were now so afraid of him that they had to have a sword to hang over his head. They had gambled on his buying Sue's safety with noninterference in their affairs.

But they hadn't really known Bill Tolliver. Whoever kidnapped the little girl had made a bad mistake. The old man would never stop until he had found his granddaughter, and the one who had been rash enough to lay violent hands upon her. Tom was certain that that would be the Black Elk.

In any event, nothing was important now except finding Sue Tolliver. Everything else could be solved afterward. Tom looked anxiously at the darkening sky. Night was coming, and darkness would hinder their efforts. Still, they had to try.

They came to the stand of pines Elaine had described and Bill Tolliver reined his horse to a stop.

"You think that hound will follow 'em?" he asked anxiously.

"I think he'd better! We'll never find the trail without him!"

They watched Smoky swing from side to side on the trail. He took his time, classifying each minute scent pocket and working on from that. He cut sharply from the trail toward a bushy green pine that grew ten feet from it. Tom saw with mounting elation that some of the branches had been broken. This must be the very pine from which Eliane had been breaking foliage when the kidnappers took Sue. Smoky looked back, and Tom waved him on.

"Take it," he said.

"You sure he's got it?" Bill grumbled.

"Bill, we have to trust him! If we go by guess, we could look for a hundred years without finding Sue."

"I know everybody in the mountains," Bill Tolliver said. "I'll find who got her, dog or no dog!"

"But we haven't time to search every cabin! Don't you—"

Tom checked himself. The old mountaineer evidently

took it for granted that whoever had kidnapped Sue would never dare harm her. Tom knew the Black Elk. Without remorse and without pity he had taken hundreds of animal lives to further his own ambitions. Even though it were a human life, he would not hesitate to take another if that meant his own safety.

"Come on!" Tom said.

Smoky had broken out of the thick pines and was heading off through the open forest. He had the scent he wanted. Providing Tom wished him to do so, he could follow it as fast as was necessary. Skirting the pines, Tom and Bill urged their horses after the dog as fast as they could travel.

In a few minutes, Smoky broke out of the trees at a fork in the trail, and faltered there. The riders reined up their horses and slid to the ground.

The men who had kidnapped Sue had probably left their horses here while they advanced on foot. While Bill examined the ground, Tom looked back down the valley trail. The trees were bare, stripped of their foliage, and there were few evergreens on the slope. The two kidnappers could have seen Sue and Elaine from this point.

"He's right," Bill grunted, straightening up. "Two horses were tethered here."

Smoky cast back and forth, with his head alternately in the air and to the earth as he worked out every faint trace of scent. Bill Tolliver looked down both branches of the trail. His horse suddenly squealed and fell to fighting the bit as the old mountaineer raised in the stirrups, and pointed.

"Thataway! One of the horses spooked down there. See where he broke the brush?"

Tom looked in the direction Bill was pointing. The brush that grew beside the trail was splintered and broken, as if some heavy creature had plunged into it.

Just then Smoky turned. With his head high in the air, he started in the opposite direction. Tom swung the pinto.

"Come on, Bill!"

"Not me. I'm a-goin' where my eyes tell me to go!"

He leaped his white horse past Tom and galloped down the other branch. For a moment Tom hesitated. There *was* broken brush; to all appearances the riders had gone in the direction Bill Tolliver had taken. Only the nose of a hound who had yet to prove his ability to follow a man on horseback disputed this. Tom swung in behind Smoky.

He was a mountain man and a hunter, and knew that there were all kinds of hound. But a good hound never lied; even though no human sense could detect any sort of a trail, if a really fine dog said the scent lay there, then it did. Tom was willing to trust Smoky. To search at random in the mountains would be hopeless.

Tom kept Pete at a walk, and watched intently. The big hound had his head up, but was certainly following a scent. The horsemen had brushed the bushes on the side of the trail and left their scent upon them. Johnny Magruder had been right!

Ten minutes later, he heard the pounding hooves of a galloping horse behind him. Bill Tolliver burst around a

185

bend in the trail and slowed his white horse. The old mountaineer shook his head.

"They didn't go that way."

"You're sure?"

"There's a stream crosses the trail a ways back, and it wasn't roiled up. Nobody has forded it lately."

Tom sensed the old man's impatience, and understood his desire for swift action. This slow walk would be intolerable to him. Nevertheless it was necessary. The fate of the little girl lay in Smoky's nose, in his ability to trace the difficult scent he was following.

The trail became narrower, and wound through thick laurel. No horse could run here without brushing his rider's legs against brush. Scent lay thicker and heavier, and Smoky broke into a run. Tom urged Pete into a pace that matched the hound's, and was aware of Bill Tolliver's big white horse pounding along behind.

They came suddenly to another fork in the trail and an abrupt halt. Here there were no trees or brush at all.

Smoky sat down, then cast in circles with his nose alternately to the ground and in the air as he sought to pick up any trace of scent. While Bill Tolliver fretted, the hound backtracked himself to make sure that he had had scent to this point. The old mountaineer slid off his horse, looped the reins over a stub, and got down on his hands and knees at the fork to look for hoof prints.

"Don't spoil the scent for Smoky," Tom warned.

"He ain't got one," Bill rumbled. "We got to move!"

As if in answer, Smoky walked straight across the intersection and up the north branch of the fork. Without hesitation, Tom rode after him. This had to be the way.

"Wait!" Bill called.

Tom halted Pete. As soon as he stopped, Smoky stopped too, and sat down in the trail. The old man was still crouched at the intersection, thinking hard.

"I know he's wrong!" he declared flatly.

"How do you know?"

"There's nothin' but wild country up that trail; whoever got Sue would take her to a cabin. There's three of 'em down the south fork and she's bound to be at one!"

"Bill, the dog is right!"

"He's wrong, I tell you."

While Tom considered, Smoky impatiently trotted ahead and snuffled at an object lying in the trail. Riding up, Tom swooped from the saddle to retrieve it. He held up a child's mitten.

"Look!"

"That's Sue's, all right!" Bill said excitedly. "That Smoky dog's sure got a nose, Tawm!"

"What now?"

"Follow him. He's been right every time."

Twilight began to fall, deepening into shades of gray. They rode on, slowly, holding their horses to a walk when Smoky slowed his pace, and letting them trot when he found the going easier.

As they went on and on, Tom tried to stifle the uneasiness he felt. This was completely wild country they were penetrating, and they had only a hound's assurance that Sue had really been brought this way. He finally reined Pete to a halt and turned in the saddle.

"What do you make of it, Bill?"

"I dunno," replied the old man's worried voice out of

187

the half-darkness. "There ain't a livable cabin within ten miles of here, as I know of."

"I think we ought to walk," Tom said. "Maybe we're pushing Smoky too fast, and it's hard to see him."

"That's too slow."

"It's better than overrunning."

"Mebbe you're right," Bill grudgingly assented.

Leading Pete, with Smoky now walking beside him, Tom went on up the trail. The night deepened. From a tree almost overhead came the hunting cry of a great horned owl, and there was a rattle of wings as a startled grouse left its perch. The rattle ceased abruptly; the owl had made its kill. Behind him, Tom heard the steady "clip-clop" of the horses' hooves on the frozen earth.

The kidnappers must have run their horses much of the way, and even so have traveled part of the way in the darkness. Tom tried to reason out exactly what they intended to do.

Many years ago there had been several cabins and clearings in this part of the mountains. Now the cabins were tumbledown and the clearings grown to trees. It was one of the wildest and most inaccessible parts of the mountains, one that only old trails penetrated. If Smoky had made no mistake, why were her kidnappers bringing little Sue Tolliver here?

Smoky stopped suddenly, and turned off the path, toward the west. The dog tensed himself, and growled faintly. A shadow in the night, the old mountaineer came up beside Tom.

"What is it?" he whispered.

"They've left the trail, and probably led their horses from here. We must be close. What's around here, Bill?"

"There ain't nothin', there ain't."

"Are you sure?"

There was a long moment of silence. "Painted catamounts!" Bill Tolliver whispered hoarsely. "The old silver mine!"

"That's it!"

Tom remembered now. He had heard his father speak of the single vein of precious ore that had been discovered in the mountains, and of the wild stampede it had caused. There had been a shaft driven deep into the side of the mountain, but within a few months the silver had played out. The cabins and houses built by hopeful seekers of wealth were now rotting piles on the ground. Tom made a quick mental calculation.

Not five miles away, the navigable Catchman River wound its slow course through mountains to far-off cities. If the Black Elk had chosen to go after beaver, he could not have found a better storage place than the old silver mine. Properly stretched furs could be held indefinitely. The Black Elk had only to bring green pelts here for curing, then at his leisure carry them over the mountains to a waiting boat or barge.

"Do you know where the mine is?" Tom whispered.

"Just about. Let me lead."

Slowly, careful to make no noise, Bill Tolliver led his big white horse through the brush. As they entered a shallow and almost treeless gully high in the mountains, a faint streak of dawn light broke in the east. Bill tied his horse to a lone aspen, and nodded at Tom, who rein-tied his pinto.

Smoky turned at an angle, and started toward a patch of aspens a third of the way up the opposite ridge. Tom snapped his fingers, and the dog stopped in his tracks.

"That's it," the old man whispered. "Let's go."

Their rifles ready, they stalked toward the aspens. Smoky walked between them, his head high, hot scent in his nostrils. Tom's own nose caught the aroma of wood smoke, and he put a restraining hand on the dog's neck.

They crept through the aspens, and came within sight of the door that enclosed the mine shaft. It had been recently fashioned out of fresh timbers. A stovepipe, thrust through the earth above the door, spewed blue smoke into the breaking day.

Tom looked around at Bill Tolliver, and the old mountaineer nodded his readiness. Tom stepped up to the door, yanked it open, and almost with the same motion leapt within the mine shaft.

He saw a dimly burning lantern upon an overturned box, blanketed figures on the floor, and felt warmth from a stove. Then he saw Cole Sellers.

The poacher had been dozing against the wall, a double-barreled shotgun across his lap. As Tom saw him, he jerked to wakefulness and raised the gun. There were two separate clicks as he cocked it, and before Tom could swing his own rifle around, he was staring down gaping barrels that seemed bigger than the mine shaft.

Then something hit Sellers in the head, he toppled sideways, and there was a thunderous roar as the shotgun discharged its load against the ceiling. A figure flung itself out of the darkness to wrap both arms around the poacher and bear him to the floor.

It was Buck Brunt!

Tom had no time to wonder what the redheaded warden was doing there. The awakening men beyond the stove were struggling out of their blankets. As he leapt forward to close with Lead Dather, he was aware of Bill Tolliver beside him. Then he felt a stinging blow on his nose, and tasted blood.

A savage joy overwhelmed him. These men were poachers, sworn enemies of every honest citizen who had a stake in the wildlife of the mountains. Beyond that, they were personal enemies, men who had tried to kill him, who had kidnapped a little girl to buy their own safety. Now they faced him, not in court in Martinton, but man to man.

Tom swung fiercely, and knocked Lead Dather back with a square right to the jaw. Lead's hand dived into the front of his shirt, and emerged holding a long knife. He lunged at Tom, then suddenly collapsed to the floor. Something had also hit him over the head.

Tom stepped back, surprised to find Buck Brunt again beside him. With joyful abandon the warden was swinging an odd-shaped club. Tom stared at it in amazement. It looked like the leg of a wild boar, even to the heavy hoof on the end.

"Get the girl," panted Buck. "Down there!" He pointed into the depths of the mine shaft.

Tom flung a hasty glance about him. Fred Larsen sprawled on the floor, apparently knocked out by Bill Tolliver. Sellers and Dather were also out of the fight.

Only Bob Magloon was left. White-faced and trembling, he crouched near the stove.

Without looking around, apparently careless of what happened to the poachers, Bill Tolliver rushed deeper into the mine shaft. Snatching up his rifle, Tom raced after him.

He passed through another part of the tunnel, where stabled horses snorted nervously and pulled at their tie ropes. A great pile of beaver pelts lay in one corner. Beyond the horses the shaft narrowed, as Tom could see by the flickering rays of a lantern ahead. There Tom caught up with Bill, who was kneeling beside a tumbled bed.

Sue Tolliver was sitting on the bed, sleepily patting Smoky's head. The big dog was crouched protectively beside her; he had faithfully followed the trail to the end. But Smoky was growling steadily, his eyes fixed on the black depths of the shaft beyond.

"The Black Elk!" Tom jerked out. "Let's get him! Smoky will watch her."

Reassured that his granddaughter was all right, Bill snatched up the lantern and followed Tom.

They were now in the part of the mine where the pay ore had begun to run out, and side shafts had been dug in an attempt to find more. They came to such a side tunnel, and stopped, uncertain which way to go.

"Get Smoky," Bill whispered. "We can't—"

There was a flash of fire down the side tunnel, and a bullet buried itself in the wall behind them. Tom dropped to the ground and fired back. He was aware of

Bill beside him, and realized that the old mountaineer had blown out the lantern.

As the echoes of the shots reverberated against the confining walls, Tom thought he heard a muffled shout. Then the echoes died away to a tomblike silence.

"Think I winged him," Tom breathed softly. "I'm going to find out."

On hands and knees they crawled forward in pitch blackness, feeling their way, careful to make no noise. On and on they went, until Tom's groping hand suddenly felt nothing ahead of him but a draft of cold air. He swung his hand around and stopped Bill.

"Feels like a vertical shaft," he whispered. "Wait."

Groping in the darkness, he found a pebble and tossed it ahead of him. He listened intently, but seconds seemed to pass before he heard the sound of splashing water far below.

There was the flicker of a match. Bill held it out over the abyss. By its feeble light they could see that the vertical shaft extended from wall to wall of the tunnel they were in. Tom remembered the muffled cry he had heard, and shuddered. His search for the Black Elk was over.

In silence they backed away from the pit and retraced their steps to pick up Sue. Bill carried her back into the room where Buck Brunt kept his watch on the four captured poachers. The red-haired warden turned an inquiring glance on them.

"Where is he?"

Tom flicked a thumb over his shoulder. "Fell down a

vertical shaft full of water," he said soberly. "Who was the Black Elk, Buck?"

"Garsoney. Didn't you know?"

"What!"

"There's no mistake. Our little crackpot nature lover was the Black Elk. He planned everything so well he almost got away with it. He was the one who sent me those phony transfer orders."

"Phony orders? But he *was* a warden. I saw his credentials."

"Those were Johnny Magruder's, which he'd altered. Garsoney got all Johnny's papers, including official stationery, that night he had him slugged in the trail and planted those boar tracks around him. This cement-stuffed boar's foot is the one they used. I knew they'd taken the papers, but stupidly thought it was just to delay Johnny's identification if anybody happened to find him. And I sure *was* stupid! When I started over the Klesa Trail on my fake assignment, Dather and Larsen got me the same way, and brought me up here."

"What did they want with you?"

"Garsoney needed an ace up his sleeve. He aimed to clean out the beaver in the mountains. Just in case something went wrong, and he was cornered, he wanted me as a hostage. They left you alone because Bill Tolliver had taken the warpath against them, and Garsoney decided to pit you against Bill. I guess he figured you'd keep each other busy enough so neither of you would get in his hair. Say, Bill, why *did* you take on this gang all by yourself?"

"Johnny talked some sense into him," Tom grinned.

"He's a better educator than either of us. By the way, Johnny's at Bill's now, holding Hank Jamieson."

"Good enough. I guess that's the lot."

Bill Tolliver had been examining the boar's-foot club while he listened. "Buck," he rumbled, "how come you wasn't tied when we busted in here?"

"I had been; they sure know how to tie knots. I couldn't wriggle loose until I got real mad, and that happened when they brought Sue in. I figured that was too much, and I'd better get busy. It took some skin off, but I did it, and was trying to get some circulation started so I could move fast when I started. Then you dropped in. My legs were still numb, but I already had the boar's foot, and decided to use it."

"I'm glad you did!" Tom said gratefully. "What now?"

"We'll take these four and Hank Jamieson in on charges of kidnapping and attempted murder. Even the comic judge at Martinton can't ignore that." Buck's eyes bored into Bob Magloon. "And if anybody wants to talk, he might get off with a light sentence. Now let's get going. I'm hungry."

Tom looked out into the brightening morning and went to the door for a deep breath of clean air. His eyes were attracted by a motion on the opposite slope. An antlered buck snorted there, a proud, wild symbol of mountain life. The buck looked about, shook its antlers, and began to feed.

Something brushed against Tom's leg, and he glanced down. Smoky was standing beside him, gazing sadly out across the valley. His nose twitched as he sniffed the morning breeze.

ABOUT THE AUTHOR

JIM KJELGAARD's first book was *Forest Patrol* (1941), based on the wilderness experiences of himself and his brother, a forest ranger. Since then he has written many others—all of them concerned with the out-of-doors. *Big Red, Irish Red,* and *Outlaw Red* are dog stories about Irish setters. *Kalak of the Ice* (a polar bear) and *Chip, the Dam Builder* (a beaver) are wild-animal stories. *Snow Dog* and *Wild Trek* describe the adventures of a trapper and his half-wild dog. *Haunt Fox* is the story both of a fox and of the dog and boy who trailed him, and *Stormy* is concerned with a wildfowl retriever and his young owner. *Fire-Hunter* is a story about prehistoric man; *Boomerang Hunter* about the equally primitive Australian aborigine. *Rebel Siege* and *Buckskin Brigade* are tales of American frontiersmen, and *Wolf Brother* presents the Indian side of "the winning of the West." The cougar-hunting *Lion Hound* and the greyhound story, *Desert Dog,* are laid in the present-day Southwest. *A Nose for Trouble* and *Trailing Trouble* are adventure mysteries centered around a game warden and his man-hunting bloodhound. The same game warden also appears in *Wildlife Cameraman* and *Hidden Trail,* stories about a young nature photographer and his dog.

JIM KJELGAARD

In these adventure stories, Jim Kjelgaard shows us the special world of animals, the wilderness, and the bonds between men and dogs. *Irish Red* and *Outlaw Red* are stories about two champion Irish setters. *Snow Dog* shows what happens when a half-wild dog crosses paths with a trapper. The cougar-hunting *Lion Hound* and the greyhound story *Desert Dog* take place in our present-day Southwest. And, *Stormy* is an extraordinary story of a boy and his devoted dog. You'll want to read all these exciting books.

☐	15456	A NOSE FOR TROUBLE	$2.50
☐	15368	HAUNT FOX	$2.25
☐	15434	BIG RED	$2.95
☐	15324	DESERT DOG	$2.50
☐	15286	IRISH RED: SON OF BIG RED	$2.50
☐	15427	LION HOUND	$2.95
☐	15339	OUTLAW RED	$2.50
☐	15365	SNOW DOG	$2.50
☐	15388	STORMY	$2.50
☐	15316	WILD TREK	$2.50

Prices and availability subject to change without notice.